THE COALVILLE WRITERS

First three years

To enid,

from

Dumitru

All proceeds of any sales of this book are to be donated to LOROS Hospice, Leicestershire, UK

Contents

Chapter 1- How a Writing Group Evolves

Fliss Middleton

I've long believed that if you have a great interest or passion for something then spending time with others who share the same interest is likely going to be enjoyable and educational too. I think the proliferation of Facebook groups and pages ranging from 'Auditors United' to 'Zookeepers Community,' is an indication that many people feel the same.

So, I had been writing in isolation for a while but longing to connect with others locally doing the same and see how we might support each other and advance our skills. I was very aware that there would be many writers further along in their writing Journey than myself. Some certainly more much more skilled than I and with actual published books when I had only a few newspaper and magazine articles to my credit. These were the people I wanted to listen to and learn from. I thought it also likely that there were people lacking confidence in their abilities when it came to expressing themselves in the written form. Perhaps I could encourage and support them in a group setting?

So…I put an advert on our local Next-door site and wrote a small piece which appeared in several community magazines. Peter contacted me and we met up for an encouraging chat which led on to arranging an initial meeting.

The invitation to the meeting drew quite a lot of people with extremely varied writing histories and successes. Some people from the first meeting didn't return for a subsequent get-together but over time we formed a core group and began to explore what we could do as a group to share and develop our writing.

This little book fulfils an ambition of mine and I'm so proud of us and what we as individuals and as a group have achieved over the last 3 years.

P.J. Huckerby

Duck eggs for sale, a chemical toilet and a free shed; dismantle it yourself and take away. A relentlessly barking dog and a BMX bike stolen right off a drive… in broad daylight! Don't get me wrong, local social media has its place. I do glance in its direction periodically. A case in point, back in 2018, I picked up a post on Nextdoor. It was posted by Felicity Middleton (Fliss), asking if anyone would be interested in joining a writing group to develop their creative skills. Well, I'm generally not predisposed to join groups. It always seems like a step into the unknown, more often or not, a step into something pretty challenging to remove yourself from once committed. It must have been one of those days when my guard was down; I don't know. Anyway, I have no excuse, and I responded to the invitation and met up with Fliss. At this point, the writer's group consisted of just myself and Fliss. We organised our first meeting in the Birch Tree and were joined by many more. Several years later, I still find myself in the group founded by Fliss; and I have to say I'm glad I remained. It has certainly developed my creative writing, and the other group members are fairly tolerable, so I guess I'll stick with The Coalville Writers Group for a while.

Macy Milldale

I joined the group as I had become a part-time empty nester and was looking for a new hobby. I had tried my hand at sewing lessons and was the only one in the class to make an oblong shaped cushion. I had dipped in and out, but mainly out, of the gym over the years, so the writing has been the only interest I have adhered to.

The group has a shared interest in supporting one another to develop writing skills. I have learned about different theories on how to write, come across words I have never heard of, and altogether learned a great deal from other writers.

I have also learned much about myself. I can write but I know I can write better. This is what keeps me attending the group. It's also a great atmosphere to be around other creative minds, intellectual thinkers and all-round compassionate people.

We have commandeered a local pub and I feel a sense of belonging to our small gathering; in the summer we can sit enjoying the last remnants of the sun and in the winter we are cosy inside.

For those of you afraid to speak publicly or intimidated by a group, give it a go; you may be pleasantly surprised…

Rosemary Blake

Lockdown was a bad time for me. My job was affecting my mental health. I resigned just as lockdown began. Usually, I find writing enjoyable but suddenly I was too miserable to put my mind to it. I needed to get out and meet people.

I went online to find writing groups. The nearest was the Coalville Writers Group but the contact's name was Felicity Middleton. 'Oh no,' I thought, 'I don't think I'll get on with a Linda Snell type.' (Archers reference there.) But I plucked up courage to email her and eventually heard back from Douglas Gilmour. Arh a good Scottish name.

They were meeting on Microsoft Teams. I found disembodied heads and distorted voices. They could see me but not hear me. I waved at them. How embarrassing. When I managed to fix the technology, I heard three women whose names I couldn't fix in my head and Pete who swivelled in his chair to show us his playthings: a pinball machine and a guitar.

It was exciting that the group trusted each other with the drafts of their works in progress. They all provided detailed and honest feedback. They were serious about this stuff! I continued to meet them, even after we gravitated to a pub. What I love about Coalville Writers is that they are friendly, usually tactful, well meaning, kind, fun people and best of all 'What you see is what you get.' Oh, and eventually I met Fliss Middleton. She is warm, lovely and down-to-earth. Nothing like Linda Snell.

Douglas Gilmour

'There is a meeting of local authors at Peppercorns Café in Abbey Park. You should go along.' I looked at my wife with a pained expression. Putting me in the category 'Local Author' was stretching it a bit. But going there put me in touch with a group of genuine and disappointingly talented local authors who were also planning to attend the inaugural Coalville Writers Group.

Here I found Peter, Fliss and my spiritual home. A disparate group of people and backgrounds at various stages of the writing process and experience. From Rosemary who has a series of books already published to others who are just trying to beat their excellent ideas into some sort of structure. The experience has been largely like taking nine cats out on a monthly walk, but everyone has enjoyed themselves and, it seems, gained from the experience.

For me, the three years has taught me to try and make every word count. So, I'll stop there.

Terri Eynon

Strap-hanging on the number 11 bus on my way home from secondary school, a friend of my mother's asked me what I wanted to be when I grew up. 'A Poet,' I replied. That didn't go down well at home. 'Poets end up starving in garrets', my Dad pointed out. He was probably right. And anyway Keats was a doctor. So was Chekhov. I was sure I could squeeze literature into my life somewhere.

I did manage some writing, here and there, and even had a few poems published. But four decades without any formal encouragement did nothing for my literary confidence. So, when Fliss said she was going to start a Writers Group, I jumped at the chance.

I enjoyed the exercises, even those that expected me to write stories instead of poems. Being given a handful of random words, or a couple of characters and a setting, gave me something to work with. Being part of a group gave me a reason to commit to the task.

I am involved with Snibston Heritage Trust who work to interpret a former mine. I have found the challenge of the exercises has helped me to find new and interesting ways to re-tell the stories of the mine and its people. I would recommend a Writers Group as a great way to build confidence, develop your skills, and make good friends in the process.

Kelly O'Shea

Arriving at the pub prior to the designated meeting time, I sat alone outside. I know one person's face from an email and I'm hoping they're here so I know which table to join. It is scary meeting new people for the first time, especially when you have no idea what they look like or where they usually sit. I saw a man eating. Another man arrived with a satchel. They began to converse. My astute judgement told me these would be two of the members. I turned out to be right! Another new member had asked inside the pub and was directed to the two gentlemen sat at the table. I tagged along feeling awkward but was made to feel welcome by the group.

I have written many things for many years, never allowing anyone to read any of it. But I have decided to try things that scare me. A crazy dream of being a published author is one of them. So, I have joined a lovely group of people in the hopes of making friends and growing as a writer.

Peter Matthews

Well, it's the start of yet another folder that will come under the writing umbrella.
I have never written a novel and don't intend to. Short stories, poetry, haiku (which I will come to), and memoirs including travel. Most of my writing has been rubbed off from life, from my running away from school to my later experiences having been retired this last thirty odd years. However, I have dropped in the occasional ghost story of the gentler kind that never hurts anyone who would be disposed to switching on the light.

I guess that I started around the year 2000 after I attended a lecture at the WEA which was called "The Song of the Shirt." Thomas Hood wrote the poem about the distressed circumstances of seamstresses in the middle of the 19th. century and being as I wasn't overly impressed with it, I decided to have a go myself. Looking at my attempt now, well, there is a feeling that it's a bit twee. So much for self-regulation.

I have been with various groups during these retirement years, all of which have disappointingly folded, latterly due to the pandemic, and so I have turned to reading groups in the county which I have found to be a boon. The introduction of

Zoom I have discovered as beneficial in that not only being introduced to new writing but also having the opportunity to read it out, I feel has given a new importance to the word and its place. It has enabled me to scan the lines of the poem or story giving emphasis or pause where I think it is required. I now appear to think differently when writing.

Regarding my joining The Coalville Writers: I thought that under the outdoor circumstances the organisers did well though some of my new fellow writers were out of sight on the other bench. Having an indoor Round Table would be too much to hope for especially as I presume it is a freebie and that the pub is hoping that you will lash out on throat lubricants.

Haiku: Originally a Japanese three line poem, the subject of it being nature, the form now spans the world in different forms. Two of mine are as below:

milk mouthed, warm smelling,
pink poised on life's lip, to lay
fed for tomorrow.

from searching children
horse chestnut seed stays hidden,
unstrung, unconquered.

Cerys Linton

This group was well developed by the time my friend introduced me to them. Although I can't say very much about the initial development, as a relative latecomer I have been pleasantly surprised at the acceptance and support and inclusivity of the group. I am a rather passive partner still, but I gain confidence and determination weekly. I marvel at the other group members talent and the places in which they shine.

The encouragement the group gives is invaluable. I honestly do not think I would have stuck with my own projects otherwise. I also feel it has helped me mature as a person as well as improve my writing, and I am an extremely introverted person who really does not do groups. I hope one day to give more back to the group and be a more active member.

Chapter 2- A Raven – The Coalville Symbol

A Coalville Raven

Terri Eynon

Corvids vary:

Jackdaws race the rooftops

tagging the streets like teenage fiends.

Crows work the canopy, their gangs

a clatter and bob of callings.

But you look down your roman nose

and stand the pit-top, settled in your weight,

dark-suited civil servant,

hands behind,

come to inspect the yield.

Harbinger of Doom?

Rosemary Blake

The raven veered upwards with a loud slapping of black wings. Avis gasped, fearful that the bird had been hit by a stone. If he had, the bird managed to escape anyway.

'Yeh, away you black beast. Devil's servant,' the tallest of a group of boys jeered.

'Come,' Avis's mother tugged on her hand, pulling her into her skirts.

Avis said, 'But the poor bird.'

'There's nothing we can do. People, especially young boys, turn on things they don't understand. It's the way it is.' Her mother bent double to cough. 'They say that ravens feed off corpses.'

Avis shivered. Her mother led her along a pathway to the heavy, wooden door of the almshouse and then down a cold, echoey corridor.

A stern woman with a square jaw appeared.

Avis's mother said, 'The squire has sent me mistress. I need help. I'm consumptive and I'm getting worse.'

The woman hmphed. 'This way. Leave your child outside. She doesn't need to be here.'

Mother gave an anguished look.

'I will be fine Mother. You just get well.'

Avis stood in the street, too shocked to cry or even to move. She leant against the wall unwilling to move far from her only relative. She remembered when Old Hester had coughed like that, and she soon died. Mother hadn't kept up payments on their cottage. Soon Avis would have no home.

She went back to their cottage to gather up as much as she could carry. It smelt of fresh rushes that mother had thrown down on the floor. She wrapped up the remains of a loaf of bread, their flint and steel for lighting a fire, a knife, a wooden bowl, and then she picked pungent herbs from the garden. She longed to speak to their neighbours, but they were struggling themselves and wouldn't be able to help.

Pulling the door behind her she said a last farewell to their home. As she left, she saw the landlord approaching. She'd escaped just in time.

Avis took a dusty track out to the heath. She shivered, overcome by fear and hollow loneliness. The land was barren apart from rocks and prickly gorse. Avis feared entering the woods in case highwaymen were hiding there. She would need to be strong to survive. Just as she was at her lowest, she heard a cough. It was a black raven, shining iridescent purple and green in the fading sun. It hopped forward to perch on a jagged rock nearby.

Girl in a Duffel Coat

P. J. Huckerby

I wonder if the Mercedes has set off yet. I guess you never allow yourself to think about it…not really. You don't let it enter your mind, certainly don't invite it in, like a vampire at your door. You banish it as if you're invincible. Pacify yourself with the trivia of life,

a shield against the inevitable. Anyway, no point dwelling; after all, it is my day.

I worked for Leadsom's for forty years or thereabouts. Most of my years there, without a company car, mean bastards. When I got the regional job, they gave me the Mondeo; I had to use the train before that. Can't complain though…but it was forty years of my life; there's no getting away from that. It all seemed vital then; it still does; I mean, everyone needs vacuum cleaner spares, don't they? …I don't know. All I remember about Leadsom's in those early days are those train journeys. Those little stations. Not the big ones like Derby and Birmingham New Street. No, the little ones on the local line. Cromford, Belper, Matlock, Ambergate and Whatstandwell. That girl in the duffle coat. She sat two rows in front of me. She always had that blue coat on, even in the summer. Such a long time ago. I bet she's in her sixties now. I wish I'd spoken to her, too scared, I guess; I felt tense and clumsy. I thought the spell would be broken if I said anything to her. I nearly did speak to her once, my heart beating right out of my chest. I looked into her eyes for a split second. Too short a moment for her to notice. But the snapshot of her face has always stayed with me; her perfect face. I just returned to my usual seat, the coward that I am. I meekly waited for my desire, her allure and tension, to dissipate as I slipped back into the refuge of fantasy and the commute humdrum. Crossing the line from my dull world into the unknown, just a step, just a step, but I was terrified. No risk in dreaming though, is there? I was pathetic, afraid my future train journeys would be eternally mortifying if she'd turned away. Seeing her sitting two rows in front of me every day would be terminally excruciating. Why is rejection so unthinkable? So I retreated to my secure imagination of her love. God now, oh now I wish I could feel my heart beat out of my chest.

I suppose the Mercedes has left now; it must have. I guess it's gone past the post office by now. I bet the bodywork is gleaming, waxed to an inch of its life and raven black.

Looking out of the window on the Derwent Valley Line all those years ago. The Amber Valley, the River Derwent and rolling hills looming up to brooding skies. I remember crows. I don't know why. They seemed to always be there, feathers waxy like the polished bodywork of that Mercedes coming to collect me. Black crows in the distance, stark trees, fleeing speckles against the ominous clouds above Duffield station. I never knew her name, the girl in the duffle coat. I think she was called Hannah or Helen, maybe Heather. It doesn't really matter; she smelled of lilies… I can smell lilies now. Her eyes were dark brown, almost black with that heavy eyeshadow and mascara, so trendy back then. Cell phone on the train, wellingtons in the rain.

The poem across my heart. I had it done at Luthor's Tattoo Emporium in Morecambe; I don't know what possessed me; I suppose it was a rare moment of madness. I've had very few of those. Just words about the love of life by some poet or other; I can't remember who. It wasn't too painful. Luthor was skilful and a careful artist. I remember thinking about the duffle coat girl when he set to work. It was only for her; the words were only for her. But soon, they will be gone, the poetry in my skin and everything.

I suppose the black Mercedes has arrived now. So soon, how short a journey, how short a life. I've had few friends; I expect a modest assembly will attend. There'll be an awkward and generic eulogy by some official I've probably never met. I imagine my truncated life will be served up speedily with no smiles, no tears. Who am I, who was I? Isn't that everyone's question? My future and end are here today. I've left the black Mercedes now. My heart remains still, but now I'm entirely outside my body; the crows are closer. The flames await, and the mysteries afar. Will my consciousness perish or ascend beyond the fire? Or will my essence join my body, turn to a few handfuls of charcoal dust, blown away, like the crow speckles over Duffield Station? Wouldn't everyone wish for more? I won't be afraid, or at least I'll try, but if I am, I'll just go back in time and remember that girl…the girl in the blue duffle coat.

The Crow

Cerys Linton

I believe us to be the repository of the dead's memories,

Of the dying memory, in living memory.

Here we are, stooping and pecking and harassing the underworld,

Still here, existing in bright black.

We'll keep your lies for you,

Really, it's no trouble.

I'll just put them neatly under my feathers, see?

Like this, like this, like so.

Much more trustworthy than the squirrel,

His tail talking diagonal while he chitters,

The pepper moth warns you of your pollution,

Flattens herself hopelessly against white tiles.

But we see her.

And you.

Dawn Chorus

Douglas Gilmour

The British Antarctic Survey (Coalville) hadn't perhaps been the obvious place to go to when the Big Freeze started. A lot of people had headed south, trying to cross the Med in boats. Then it froze over, and you could walk it, which brought its own problems. More stayed put, and died where they were, once the gas stopped flowing. Sue grimaced at the thought of the brief but brutal Calor Gas wars. It had been the last large-scale action before everyone who could go had gone and everyone that couldn't was holed up somewhere or dead.

Bob, though, said they had a full Antarctic Base at the site, for crew practice and trying out new ideas. Some sort of development grant for the East Midlands. There had been thirty-one of them when they set out; twenty-four of them had found out Bob had been right, nineteen of them by the time they had made the place their own. Bob had been the last to go, frostbite.

They had been holed up here for fourteen months now. The year that had no summer was followed by a winter that knew no sun.

'Do you know what day it is?' Sue asked. Steve was the only other person in the upper deck of the habitation module, but he still looked surprised at being talked to.

'I don't know, Tuesday,' he replied looking reluctantly over the top of his paperback.

'It's the 21st of June,' Sue replied.

'And...?'

‘Midsummer,’ said Sue. Steve laughed and went back to his book. ‘The reason why I bring it up is because the crows are back.’ I pointed out of the triangular windows to the shapes moving among the black trees beyond the snowfield that used to be the carpark.

‘Mmm,’ said Steve, firmly disengaged. Giving up the silent struggle Sue passed the rest of the guys doing a speed trial on the climbing wall and walked through two modules before getting to an exit. Sue pulled on the salopettes and parka and picked up the shotgun without really thinking about it. Ever since something had eaten Dave everyone had polar bear on their mind because in many ways the alternative was worse.

She tugged open the airlock and made the short drop to the snow. They really had to get a clearing detail up or learn how to jack the modules out of the pack.

The air was still, so although bitter, Sue didn’t get that sense of her life ebbing away on a timer as soon as she was out the module. Now that she was clear of the hum of the habitation she could hear the crows. It was somehow shocking. Life outside. They seemed excited, circling around their favourite trees. Beyond, Sue had clear line of sight to the horizon. Whereas the sky had just been varying degrees of grey cloud before, there was a brighter patch, a gold zone hinting at the sun unseen for more than a year. And it broke through, a great red eye bursting through. The crows called their harsh dawn chorus triumphantly. Summer was coming.

The Raven

Macy Milldale

The raven scavenges the roadkill. Sharp, jolty movements, tearing the fur. The shiny black feathers look pristine. The bird keeps checking for movement around him before ripping off more flesh. Darting back and forth for the next morsel.

My thoughts and memories are also jolting me. Tearing through my mind, fragments: morsels. Meaningless images that I am unable to piece together. Inconsequential random thoughts. Not at all how I thought it would be.

The raven entertains me and focuses my attention away from any intrusive doubts. No, I am perfectly clear. My resolve is absolute. Dementia, no that wasn't in my retirement plan. I am not going to end up a burden on my family and have everything I worked so hard for taken from me to pay for some young carer to sit me on a commode four times a day. Locked in a mind that makes no sense. Surrounded by family I don't recognise. It's getting worse, I can picture my husband's face sighing at me and the deep cut worry lines on his forehead.

I begin to drift and my eyes are heavy. My breathing is shallow but I have never felt calmer.

The raven pecks quickly now as a car approaches. Then swoops up and away into the darkening clouds.

I am sad he has departed. It was the least lonely I have felt for some time.

I look at the scraps of roadkill. What could it have been? It reminds me of me. A fragment, unrecognisable mash.

I am content to close my eyes. There is nothing more worth looking at.

A Reaper and his Raven

Kelly O'Shea

Taking the brown manilla file with today's contracts in it, I wondered how many souls I will be taking today. Opening it up there was just one. One file, this hadn't happened in…in…well actually I can't remember the last time I only had one file. I could put this down to our recent…mishap, but I'm trying not to overthink situations anymore. I heard overthinking is bad for your mental health. I guess this will be a nice easy day and we'll be back home before we know it. Ray and I leave nice and early; may as well get it over and done with.

It isn't for everyone, soul reaping. We have been called many names over the years: Death, La Muerte, Joe Black and the Grim Reaper. But actually my name is Barry, and there is a whole organisation of reapers, not just one. I mean really, how do people think one person could be everywhere, all the time, every minute of the day working? No, I clock in and clock out like everyone else. Well, maybe not everyone. Of course, there is Hunter. I swear that isn't his actual name. He struts into the office, hands in the air, swirling his scythe around and making a massive show of his ever-present self! Piss off Hunter. He has the most souls reaped of everyone and gets all the good jobs. I wanted Marilyn Monroe, but no, it went to Mr Thinks-with-his-trouser-scythe Hunter. He makes me sick. I skulk out of the office before he arrives. I just can't handle his bullshit today.

Ray flies on ahead, no point having a harbinger of death arrive after Death now is there? I arrive at the unassuming single-story property. Flowers fill the front garden, I touch a couple and they wilt and dry, my calling card. Yes, it might be cheesy but I have to have some pleasures.

‘He’s on the kitchen floor.’

‘What? We’re not bloody late are we? Did Captain Twatface get here first?’

‘No, no.’ Ray looks down. ‘This one’s a dog.’

‘A bloody dog? Not again, why have we been relegated to animals?’ Ray lowers his beak and gives me the stink eye. ‘Oh yeah, Betty Whyte. Shit. I’m sorry, okay? How many more times am I going to have to say I’m sorry? I’m a fan. I just went to see her, and I fell. Look we’ve all made mistakes. No-one is still pissy at Colin for taking out Michael Jackson! He was the actual King of Pop, but nooo, I have ONE accident, kill ONE little old lady and its pet cemetery for eternity. Let’s just get this over and bloody done with.’

Griffin Crow Mansion

Dumitru Langham

This is your Master speaking … oh, okay enough of the creepy voice! Let's try this again…greetings, this is your master here…Yes, it I, Dumitru, your slightly zany writer, back with another short story which is on the theme of crows, which in case you haven't noticed, our book cover is image of crow, of which the raven cousin is linked to our town heritage! So, let's get this story started; as an urban/contemporary fantasy writer my job is to guide you through my world which is more complex than spaghetti junction!

They say every neighbourhood has a creepy, creaky old house at the end of the street, the one that not even the cool kids dare approach. Now, let's imagine a creepy, creaky old house in the middle of the countryside surrounded by rolling fields, and old oak trees tall enough to hide it from public view. That's what our character saw when they arrived at this strange mansion which might not look all that seems. Overgrown and shabby.

It was late October when Kai, a light tan sixteen year old elf, his little sister and his dad, arrived at this mansion. Kai's dad refurbished houses for a living. All around leaves were orange and red, a blaze like sunset. The mansion was very shabby and scruffy, and the front was shaped like beak of bird which of course is very unusual for a manor house. The only creature around was a griffin the size of domestic cat, sitting in the tree. It had the rear legs and tail of cat but the claws, head and beak of a shabby crow. It let out an eerie call. I know you might think that this is starting to sounded like horror, but actually this story is…. Well, you're going to have to keep reading to find out.

"Well kids," said Dad, his ears pricking up with excitement. Kai and his little sister looked dispirited at the unkempt house, which had the strong smell of cat.

"Are you sure this inheritance is not someone pranking us dad?" Kai asked, looking around the dining hall, around which all the statues of griffin crows probably explained the beak shape at the front of the manor!

"Look at this way kids, it's all part of adventure…. That's what gran would have wanted," said Dad. Half-heartedly Kai rolled and pulled his baggy loose hoodie over his head and hitched his track suit sweat bottoms a little higher as he began to take in the run-down house. He missed that one of the ornamental griffin crows was a real one from outside, following him around, but every time Kai looked, the crow just sat still and blended right in to the crazy house's ornamentation.

"Hey Kai?" Kai's little sister asked, holding her stuffed unicorn protectively. "Can you check out the toilet? I hear something."

"Oh, whatever," said Kai but something in his sister's voice made him go and have a look. As he changed direction, he saw the crow. It gave him looked as if say, 'I've come for you'. Filled with a sense of doom, Kai squawked and backed into his sister.

"Griffin!" Kai squeaked.

"Troll!" his sister squeaked back. Kai twisted round. A troll's hand was reaching out of the toilet, reaching out for his little sister! Kai wanted to shout for his dad, but was frightened that if he did, the troll, or his hand, would know where they both were. The griffin swooped, passed over both elves and bit the most outstretched finger, and backed out of the room again. With a pop, the trolls hand collapsed like a boneless frog. Most of it fell inside the toilet but a lot of it splatted on the floor. The smell was really bad.

"You found it, you have to clean it," said Kai quickly and he ran off to find where the griffin crow had gone.

So, have you worked out the meaning of this story? No? Well, the fact is, that the crow is a creature associated with magic, not just a creature of bad omen!

Chapter 3- Random Prompts/Words Developed into Stories

The poem *Armchair* was inspired by a home-made card game. The task was to write a short piece that connected one abstract concept – such as depression, youth, time – with a physical thing – such as blackberries, a hammer, an armchair.

Working random words into a story – castle drawbridge, mouse or rat, lightning, parachute and eating – led to *Walking through my Life and Others, A Jump into the Unknown* and *A Tiny Act of Bravery*.

A historical random story generator set the following task: When a perceptive stable boy and a free-spirited cloth-maker are torn apart by the decline of the Tang dynasty, one of them must trust the other to do the right thing until at last they can be together. This led to the tale *Red Beans*.

Using a different random story generator, in a contemporary setting with a protagonist who is lovable but haunted, we were tasked to create a puzzling tale of ambition and growing up in which they will be forced to forge a new identity so that nothing will ever be the same again. This brief led to the intriguing title *Huītzilōpōchtli can wait*.

Asked to write a conversation in a café, or write about a thing, or write about a funeral, one author chose to combine all three prompts into the final story in this section, *A Café, a thing and a funeral.*

Armchair

Terri Eynon

Upholstered once upon a time, it wears

its history now;

not uniformly grey

the broad arms bear the scars

of coffee spilt

the tragedies of late-night cheese and these

the crumbs of you I dare not sweep away,

the slight depression where you used to sit

where, if I sank, I'd not get out of it.

Walking through my life and others.

Cerys Linton

I walked with the dogs to the field and met a man also walking his dog along the way. It seemed that he could not stop talking. Words flowed quietly from his mouth without apparent volition, movement or breath. However, what he said was all very sensible, kind and reasonable, and dwelt mainly on his affection for his dog and the best way to treat them generally. In due course, another walker arrived with her dog. All four dogs together suddenly made a tumultuous mass of noise and chaos and near violence, but the man continued his gentle unstoppable discourse, as if the scene was entirely different in his head to the one before him.

Suddenly he stopped completely and the woman dog walker, who I think knew him, filled the unexpected space. She said her holiday had been cancelled, but she would hopefully go the next week. She said that she had done all her housework and chores, including cleaning out the fish tank, but that she was not worried, because if she died on holiday, things would still get done, just not as well. She also said she had made a five-layer meringue cake for the holiday park team, but said she was not worried about the cancellation, because the cake would freeze very well. I marvelled at my good fortune in meeting people of such kindness and innate beauty.

I could not help wondering how the cake would fit in the freezer, and what the mechanics of transporting it to the holiday park might be, how she would give it to them, and I wondered to myself if a pizza may have been a more practical choice, from everybody's point of view. But still, I have never made a cake of any layers, for anybody, and while very busy and perhaps with a great deal on her mind she had done so.

Talk of food seemed to prompt the man to talk again, and he made a connection in his head to some terriers he had witnessed chasing a rat earlier, in the adjoining field. He said that the terriers, as their name would suggest, had terrified the rat so much, it had died of fright and he had seen it frozen with fear, on its back with its feet with its hands up. The terriers had then lost their appetite apparently and left it. He said it was as big as a cat. I cheerfully dismissed the whole tale as apocryphal.

I walked on after wishing the man and the woman well, and eventually discovered the rat lying on the path in plain view. The man had been completely truthful and correct. Not only kind and reasonable, he was also honest. The rat was indeed as big as a cat, dead, with its hands up, although I thought its expression was baffled rather than terrified, but maybe its fear had changed to bafflement as it died.

I arrived home with the dogs, and my sister called, to inform me that huge spiders had been deliberately parachuting down on my spider-phobic niece's face all night, to scare her out of her wits. I thought that this was also an exaggeration of some kind, till I realised, why else would they do it? I closed the call quickly, as I saw one of my foster dogs was dragging a huge mass of carrier bags out of the shed. A large hedgehog spilled out of the bags, and from the smell I thought it was surely dead from suffocation, sleeping mistakenly in drowsy warm plastic, and I cursed the lack of proper recycling facilities, and my own laziness.

The hedgehog slowly revived, started to breathe again, and as I provided him with a new place to rest, in a few old housecoats, I considered the making of a secure hedgehog environment, with perhaps a hedgehog operated portcullis. That night, a bolt of lightning awoke me from a nightmare of serial hedgehog murders. The culprit was found to be a deeply traumatised rat.

Jump into the Unknown

K.H Parks

Paloma walked towards the drop zone in her black jumpsuit, helmet and goggles, all her senses tingling with excitement and dread. She had met her friends, who were coming to watch her from the safety of the ground, in the clubhouse. Emma had ordered pizza for lunch and Kirsty had shared a few slices, but Paloma could eat none of it. She had just managed an energy bar earlier that morning but now her stomach was churning. The butterflies she had started the day with had turned into swooping pterodactyls.

Emma had sworn never to try such a pursuit as skydiving. She had served in the forces and now said: 'It all depends on how well the person packing your parachute does it. You don't want to be at the mercy of someone who misses something.' Her words hung on the air ominously.

Paloma reasoned that Emma's days in the forces had preceded the age of health and safety mania. You could barely take a night class these days at the local community centre without a risk assessment being required. She carried this assurance with her on the day.

Paloma had opted for the tandem skydive this first time, thereby eliminating the necessity to take that step herself over the edge to plunge alone out of a small aircraft. She would be strapped to Kevin, the experienced instructor, who leered at Paloma in what he clearly thought was a friendly manner. Finally, their call came, and they all trooped purposefully towards the small plane; several of them, Paloma included couldn't resist a leap into the air, whooping with joy.

As they approached the aircraft, Paloma noticed it was very small with sliding doors. The noise of the engines was deafening and the smell of diesel quite overpowering as they all sat there in their seats, climbing to 14,000 ft. The plane certainly seemed to labour a little as it climbed the ascent. When their turn came, Kevin asked her, cheerfully, if she was alright. She nodded decisively. Cancer Research, her chosen charity would be glad of the funds, she told herself, as they edged out of the plane. Paloma pulled on the harness straps, testing their strength.

The moment came at last as they descended into freefall and Paloma caught her breath as she felt like she had left her belly behind on the plane. The wind whooshed and she cried out in hysterical terror, travelling at 120 mph as the adrenaline fired through her blood. It really was like flying, albeit swiftly towards earth. She gazed upwards at the clouds, which were beautiful.

At 6,000 ft Kevin eventually pulled the toggle to deploy the parachute and they floated down. Suddenly the wind picked up and Paloma gulped as they were blown off course. They were near a castle now and Paloma saw its portcullis glinting as its spikes descended in the sunlight. She noticed a rat scurry across the courtyard and squirmed in distaste. She started as thunder suddenly rumbled. A few minutes later lightning flashed. Surely, they would not have scheduled the jump in these conditions, was the thought which pounded through her brain as their parachute plummeted rapidly towards some trees. Paloma screamed now, unable to contain her terror any longer, as she fell down, down to destruction below…except she wasn't falling, she was sitting up in bed, her heart racing, whilst she gasped for breath. She hoped this wasn't a premonition for the real thing.

The Monolith

Douglas Gilmour

The bright summer sun streamed into the Old Bean on the Shore Road while Andy picked up his cappuccino and millionaire shortbread and spotted Peter Campbell. Despite the weather Peter had still managed to find a shadowy corner of the café to hole up. Only when sitting did Andy notice the grandfather clock taking up a seat space between them.

‘Is he with you?’ Andy asked. Peter looked suspiciously at the clock.

‘Yes, I was hoping you could give me a hand with it back to the house.’

‘Do you not think it a bit irresponsible to take a clock for a walk on the assumption that, if you get a bit tired, you can rope in a stranger to help you get it back?’ asked Andy.

‘You’re not a stranger. And you are always in here about three,’ stated Peter. They both looked at the grandfather clock for confirmation that it was indeed just passed three.

‘Why not just wear a watch like everyone else?’

‘No, you’re not seeing the big picture. I had my Aunt’s funeral today over in Balloch.’

‘I’m sorry to hear that. Were you close?’

‘Not so handy since we moved to Helensburgh but I still popped in every now and then. You know, when I could.’ Peter took a sip from his tall skinny latte. 'But anyway, the wake was at the house. Well, I say wake, but it was more like a fire sale with the Macgregor side of the family playing true to form. And I knew my sister always had an eye on this thing.'

'And you have saved it for her? Snatched the clock from the teeth of the MacGregor's as it were.'

'Something like that, yes.'

'It's like the old clan wars all over again.' Andy's eyes were defocused now as he strode across the mist covered heather, shield on his arm, broadsword in his hand, a warm welcome waiting for him when…

'I've seen that look before. You've never been further north than Luss,' said Peter sharply.

Andy drew breath to protest. 'I know a great deal about Highland history.'

'Watching Braveheart ten times does not count. The point is I need to get this clock somewhere safe before my sister sees it.'

'In order to not spoil the surprise.' Andy tapped the side of his nose and attempted a wink.

'Eh? Ah, yes. No, no not really. Andy, you see I was always terrified of this thing when I was a kid. It was a big creepy house and this clock always seemed to be the dark, cold centre of my Aunt's home. When we were playing hide and seek she would invariably hide in this thing.'

'There is space for a wee child right enough,' confirmed Andy.

‘I knew she was in there, but I was so afraid of the clock I couldn’t bear to get close enough to find her. She always won, every bloody game.’

‘So what are you going to do with it?’ asked Andy tying up the empty sugar straw into a neat bow.

‘Break it up with an axe when I get home. She can’t hide in it then.’ Andy couldn’t help thinking that the chances of Peter’s sister hiding in anything smaller than a minibus these days were slim and was about to say so when the clock struck for the half hour.

The single bell rolled out from the clock, crushing all chatter in the café, confirming the fleetingness of joy. Beyond the open doors the gulls abandoned their chip papers, took flight, silently fleeing back to the safety of the sea. The sun dimmed, for winter had returned with that sound. As the toll and its echo finally faded, the café seemed drawn in, hopeless supplicants to the dark wood monolith looming in the corner. Children hushed on hearing the ticking advance of death for the first time. Andy reached up a hand to touch the case.

‘Maybe just give it your sister, eh?’

A Tiny Act of Bravery

Rosemary Blake

Sitting in her workroom looking glumly at the sewing machine, Rachel did not feel like working. She reviewed her orders. She'd managed to turn up some curtains and altered a skirt, but she couldn't bring herself to make a start on Amanda Cattermole's wedding dress. She had called Amanda to make excuses. Amanda didn't want to find another dressmaker, but she accepted that Rachel needed time. Rachel sighed and clicked off the phone.

Nothing could release her from flashbacks of Jasper being hit by lightning. She could see his mangled and singed body surrounded by burned grass. How dare people carry on when Rachel and Jasper couldn't? It was no good, she couldn't continue as she was. She drew all the blinds pulling up the drawbridge between herself and the world.

Silently rocking in her chair, the gnawing in Rachel's stomach roused her to move. She had been avoiding the kitchen with its hard flooring and harsh lighting but now she made herself switch off the fluorescent lights and enter the darkened room. The fridge was almost empty apart from a pack of butter and a carton of foul-smelling milk. Turning to a cupboard, she squatted to explore its furthest reaches. Ha – a couple of packets of biscuits and an Easter egg. Jasper had probably squirreled the treats away. She decided to believe that they were his last present to her. She sank to the floor and devoured the Easter egg, comforted by soft chocolate melting on her tongue and teeth.

The thought of Jasper at Easter made her cry. As streetlights appeared through the window, the outlines of the kitchen turned golden. She caught a movement. Rachel hadn't noticed a presence until a grey mouse skittered right across her eyeline. It stopped, sat up and sniffed the air but the moment Rachel shifted, the mouse disappeared through a tiny gap.

Could Jasper have returned in the form of a mouse?

Rachel spent the following weeks sitting on the floor surrounded by scattered biscuit crumbs. She learned to be still so that the mouse grew in confidence and ventured nearer. She felt a glow of companionship.

Amanda Cattermole's dress sat accusingly in its box in her workroom. It was a treasured vintage wedding dress which Amanda's fiancé's grandmother had made from parachute silk during the war. If anyone could revamp it Rachel could, but Amanda had begun to text every few days. Rachel ignored the texts. She lifted the dress out of its box. At least it hadn't yellowed. She held it to her chest and stroked the material, unable to control her tears.

The mouse was waiting in the kitchen. He had to be brave to survive and Rachel realised that so did she. She took a deep breath and stood up a little straighter. With barely any hesitation she collected up the boxed wedding dress, opened the door and marched outside. The fresh air was bracing as Rachel delivered the dress to Amanda's doorstep.

Red beans

Terri Eynon

Xin Quji dozed quietly now as the morning scent of peach blossom drifted in through the tavern window. The ferry's rough clamour of ropes and creaking timber had woken him to a sweat of remembered fear. Calm once again, he stretched, easing his scarred left leg into a better position on the thin mattress. It had been a strange arrival. He twisted the precious hairpin in his hand, feeling the familiar knots under his calloused weaver's fingers.

What was the stable boy's name? Liu Xi, that was it. A thief and a liar, with a voice like a love maiden. 'Heaven is forever young,' he had sung, unloading the weaver's mare, lifting the precious cargo of sachets and silks out of her huge panniers. 'Love never gives up', the next line, they had sung together. As if nothing had ever happened. As if fourteen years had not severed him from his youth, his love and all things familiar, leaving him cowering far from Canton in a merchant's monastery, waiting for his wounds to heal. All war is cruel and civil war is the worst of all.

As he rose and dressed, Xin found himself humming the next two lines. How had the boy come by it? The hairpin, grubby but familiar, clipped to his tunic like a badge. He would have known it anywhere. He held its twin in his weaver's hands and turned it over. He knew every woven knot and shivered, remembering their last day together.

She had been afraid for him, with his Arab good looks, apprenticed to a foreigner to boot. Her hair had been black then, falling from its childish knot after an afternoon of tumbling kisses. Would it still be black now? The boy, Liu, had promised to take him to her. He even knew her name. Had said 'I will take you to where Nalan Xingde resides'. But the look in his all too familiar eyes had been hard. The liar.

Even so, he dressed and went downstairs. The willow mist had drifted from the ferry port and the eastern beach now sparkled with sunshine, belying the earlier darkness. 'Parted are the precious hairpins,' she had quoted. 'I will wet white silk as I wait for you'. And indeed, her tears had splashed on her dress when he tied the string of red beans around her wrist. And he had left. Where was she now?

Xin followed the boy through the jostling streets. This stable lad wouldn't even have been born when Huang Chao's rebel army hounded the foreign merchants out of Canton. What could he know about love and sorrow?

Stopping by a door in the wall, 'She is in here,' the boy said, dropping his eyes.

'In here?' Xin repeated. 'But this is a garden'.

'It is my mother's garden,' the boy replied.

As he stepped through the wall into the perfumed oasis Xin's head swirled. His ears filled with a drumming sound, like the sound of feet running, like water falling, like everything falling away. The boy took his arm to steady him, and they stood together looking down at Nalan Xingde's little patch of ground, bright with spring flowers.

'Did she teach you that song?' Xin Quji asked.

The boy nodded.

‘Sing it again’ he commanded.

Holding Xin’s eyes in a solemn gaze the boy sang softly ‘My heart is bound like a net, with a thousand knots inside’.

Xin looked down at his hands. He had been holding the twin hairpin so tightly the woven knots had patterned his palm. My heart is bound to you, Liu Xi, he vowed. I will not run away from here again.

Huītzilōpōchtli can wait

Douglas Gilmour

They walked away from the film club stepping over the impromptu stream flowing down Matheson Road. The noise of the rain on their umbrella made precious conversation impossible. As they walked Fats watched the deluge bounce back up and claim his jeans to his knees.

'Damn it!' He handed the brolly to Kirsten, dashed back ten paces to pick something from the pavement and then ran back to their fragile shelter. But the damage was done, he was soaked to the skin. Well, even more soaked.

The heat and steam of the Old Bean café kept the raging night at bay. Safely inside, a shallow pool spread slowly from the draining Fats as he tried to nurse warmth out of a cappuccino.

'So,' said Kirsten, 'You risked pneumonia for what?'

'A rubber band,' answered Fats.

'Okay, that makes perfect sense.' Fats felt his usual fear of ridicule nearly overwhelm him, but her smile nudged him on.

'No, you see, I get two points for picking up a rubber band. I lose one point if I walk past one and I don't see it. But I'm docked ten points if I see it and don't pick it up. And tonight I felt I needed all the points I could get.'

'Who counts the ones you don't see?' Kirsten raised an eyebrow into a cloud of red ringlets that Pixar would have been proud of.

‘Fate.’

‘Does it work?’

‘Here you are.’ Fats felt pleased with his irrefutable proof. Kirsten laughed and all Fats could think about was how he could get her to make that marvellous sound again.

‘No room for self-determination then. I was powerless in the face of your rubber band collection,’ stated Kirsten.

‘Absolutely,’ his more confident smile a mirror of hers.

‘What happens if your score goes negative?’

‘Bad things, building up to the End of Days.’

‘I can see why you had to run back. You know the Aztecs would sacrifice people to Huītzilōpōchtli to make sure that the sun would rise. Thousands would be killed to avoid the end of the world. And yet when they stopped chopping people up the sun still rose.’

‘Yeah but smallpox and firearms nearly did the trick.’

‘Granted but the sun did rise…’ Kirsten was much closer now, though neither of them seemed to have moved. ‘Why are you called Fats?’ Kirsten drummed out a Formica Boogie-woogie as part of the question.

‘I used to eat a lot of pizza. So it kind of worked both ways.’

She chuckled that wonderful laugh again. ‘What’s your real name?’

‘Kenny,’ said Kenny.

‘Oh bloody hell -- Kirsty and Kenny. That’s going to take some getting used to.’

‘No, I think it works,’ said Kenny who had been practicing saying it a hundred times a night.

‘We’ll see. Kenny?’

‘Yes.’

‘Normally when people are this close they kiss.’

‘You are so near your eyes have become one. You look like a cyclops. I wonder if that’s…’ Their lips came together. ‘Oh,’ said Kenny quietly.

The old U2 song ‘I will follow’ came to Kenny as he floated out of town on his way home. The clouds had cleared and the full moon lit up the silver road, but Fate’s rubber bands went unclaimed as he shared his joy with the heavens. Huītzilōpōchtli could wait.

Chapter 4- Waking in Unusual Clothing

Sometimes, coming up with an idea for a topic feels as hard as getting a story started in itself. As a group we have tried things, games and even colours. In this case somebody suggested 'Waking up in unusual clothing.' Which got everyone smiling and thinking.

In this case, although there was a strong set of entertaining stories created, some were closer to anecdotes than an actual story. In the end few writers selected their story for inclusion here but I'm glad they did. They are both worth a read for very different reasons.

Blouses Abduction

Dumitru Langham

Have you ever had that feeling? You know after a weird dream? What the heck was that all about? Or if you've been out on the town and had one too many? I suppose that's how I felt after I woke up being dazzled by a strange bright light, the light so bright it made me screw up my eyes. So, I suppose no-one would believe me if I told the story I am about to tell.

All I can remember is that I was on a hard surface almost like a table and felt a breeze as if there was a draught blowing through. I felt heavy, like a sack of potatoes. Okay, okay; so, I am on this table and feel naked. I begin to feel about to see if there's any clothing which, thankfully, I had. Yet it felt different. Almost like I was a bit more exposed than usual. As a man, I'm used to jeans, nice shirt and casual clothes. But before I could work out more of my unusual clothing, I was approached by some strange beings. They were grey with bald heads, wide black eyes like black holes. But they seemed to be smiling. Well, it was hard to tell as they had very small mouths yet, by the way they were shaking with what I assumed was laughter, it seemed that something was amusing them. Probably they thought they had abducted a cow, yet found some naked human on their table. Just felt something for a horrible moment – I thought they were going to shove a probe up my behind! I felt very exposed like a slab of chicken.

So, I was telling my friend the story. He was looking at me with some degree of concern and pity. I am pretty sure he was thinking the stag-do we went on last night had hit me hard.

'Okay,' said Michael, the husband to be, unable to conceal a grin. 'Are you sure that no one had spiked your drink?' At this point I needed to decide whether to continue and make myself look even more stupid or try and convince him that I had managed to get abducted by aliens.

So, back on the UFO, I had decided to find out what was amusing these little aliens. I had to blink to make sure that I wasn't dreaming. I was wearing a woman's blouse… that's right a woman's blouse. I hadn't remembered how and why I was wearing this stupid blouse. So, as you probably heard I was out on a stag-do with a good mate of mine. As I am sure you're aware these dos can get a little messy. As part of my mate's do, we wanted to dress up as women. Why? I don't know! All I can remember is I was as drunk as a skunk. The last thing I remember was a bright light which I thought was a car or truck headlight. So there you have it, that's my story I was abducted by aliens amused that I was wearing a blouse.

Blank

Peter Huckerby

Blank, void…nothing. I say nothing; I mean nothing in my head, nothing at all. You have to understand. People say, 'my mind's a total blank,' but that's not exactly true, is it? Not in most situations anyway, at least not in the same way I felt. They say nature deplores a vacuum, and I have to say that is true at least. Anyhow, it was summer when I found myself lying alone in a wheat field. I had no recollection of how I got there. I had no idea who I was. I could see the blue sky and clouds above me, feel the warmth of summer, and smell the wheat as it gently swayed around me. Yet I was numb, impassive, fixed to the ground as though I was made of lead. My eyes felt heavy, and my bones felt heavy. I watched the clouds distort and mutate, changing from one ethereal form to another; they showed nothing, revealed no clue to who I was or who I may have been. My senses were ravenous for information, hungry for anything to feed my vacuous mind.

I wasn't scared, at least not at first; numb, I suppose. I tried to move my head. The slightest effort exhausted me to the core. My brain seeking out recall sapped any scrap of energy I could muster. My empty head fell back into the harvest shadows. I gazed again at the clouds and stretched my ears to the syncopated beat of far-away machinery, a sound I dismissed for more pressing concerns. Yet I thought maybe my memory would return to me if I closed my eyes, just for a moment. I lay still for an hour, maybe two, I don't know exactly. Don't you agree, you know, how extraordinary the allure of sleep can be, how it seduces you, how it can overrule the most crucial of anxieties?

When my consciousness returned, I managed to heave myself onto my elbows and seek practical answers to my situation and condition. Figure out if I'd been hurt; look for signs of injury, bruising, and blood. It was to my surprise…bordering on horror, to find myself wearing a blush pink taffeta evening dress. A ballgown of definite quality, in fact, complete with a voluminous net underskirt. I was also wearing a diamond necklace and bracclet. I may be no expert, but this looked like lavish attire, expensive couture. This was my first clue, at least in an eliminative way. I mean, I knew for sure I was a man; yet this posed the question…why was I wearing a dress, a dress of such quality? Anxiety for my state of mental oblivion had shifted to a pettier concern. Embarrassment, and, above all, my primal vulnerability had taken centre stage. It was ridiculous that such trivial emotions had ousted the terror of amnesia. I questioned my own sense of proportion and what kind of person I was. I wondered where I was, what I would do next, where I would go. Nothing I knew lay outside the small world I had found myself in. I knew nothing further than the blue summer sky and ochre wheat that sheltered me from the mysteries beyond.

I prayed for my persona, my essence, to come home. I would welcome myself with open arms. *What a strange thought,* I told myself. I could have fallen back to the ground and waited for the daylight to yield to the velvet of night and stars, cradled safely within the wheat, secure in its embrace. But the machinery noise grew, becoming discordant, grinding louder and closer…much closer.

I don't know how I managed to stand; maybe it was the diesel fumes. Perhaps the dissonant sound of the beating engine. Maybe the violent rotating machinery had discharged a rush of self-preservation adrenaline into my veins.

The combined harvester stopped inches away from me. I watched as the spinning thresher spikes slowed to a stop. The driver, a young man in a stained Adidas hoody, jumped to the ground. 'What the fuck. You could have got yourself killed,' he yelled.

He looked at me; he looked at my dress.

'Where the hell, what the…Where have you come from? Look, I don't judge mate, but you can.... Look, don't get me wrong. I'm an open-minded bloke, but you can do that sort of thing somewhere else, just not in my field. You could have got killed.' He looked around. 'Are there any more of you lot lurking around here? This is not a bloody playground.'

'I don't know…no, I don't think so,' I said. 'Just me.'

He looked at me again but this time right into my face, almost leering. I stepped back.

'My god Tom. Tom, is that you?' he asked.

'I don't…'

'Where've you been…the police, everyone? Over a year, where the hell have you been?'

A Reality Check

Rosemary Blake

I'd always been a show off. At three, I was doing little dances for the relatives when they came around for tea, ending in a curtsey. I took drama GCSE, but that's as far as it went. I wondered if my big break had arrived when I heard they were looking for extras for a historical drama based down by the docks. So I went down there hoping to speak to the Casting Director. Just my luck, I didn't get to speak to anyone. I felt dejected. All that effort for nothing. When some of the people hanging around the set suggested we got to know each other and had a little party it appealed to my sense of adventure. I thought, *'Well why not?'*

Next thing I knew, I was sitting with closed eyes. I felt heavy. Clothes restricted my breathing. My breasts were squashed. The coat was too tight. I forced my eyelids open to discover I was wearing a red coat, shiny brass buttons down the front and extremely unflattering dark trousers. Prickly, not nice at all. What was going on? I didn't remember being at a fancy-dress party. If I had to go back to the 19th century, I would at least prefer an elegant silk dress, not this uniform. I started to unbutton it, until I realized that I was only wearing a rough linen vest underneath. How many fancy-dress outfits include the appropriate underwear? I told myself to breathe deeply to process what was happening a little at a time.

Second thoughts on the breathing. There was a steaming pile of horse muck on the street. I was on the steps of a townhouse. My head had been lolling against its gatepost. The road was eerily quiet apart from the cooing of a pigeon on the roof. If only there were someone I could ask. No cars, no passing postman.

A bunch of rowdy men appeared on the corner wearing the same daft outfit as me. I was trying to frame questions for them, when one spoke.

'Here's a likely lad. Another of Raglan's army. No good sitting there.'

'I'm sorry?'

They ignored that. One of them grabbed me under the arm.

'Come on no tarrying. You'd better have done all your carousing. We're sailing tomorrow.'

I needed to take control. 'Look, I don't know what you're talking about. And I'm not a lad. I'm a girl.'

This unfortunately led to hilarity. I was dragged from the step and roughly carried along the street. Perhaps I was dreaming, but everything was too real. A horse-drawn carriage thundered past throwing up clouds of dust. I could scarcely walk for coughing. Now I realized this was no fancy-dress escapade.

My heart raced. Sweat tickled my forehead. I attempted to think quickly, ready for anything. Why couldn't I remember what had happened before I went to sleep? Perhaps I'd been drugged or was I drunk? He'd mentioned Raglan's army. What was that? They wore red coats, so that would be pre-World War I soldiers. Boer War or Crimea. I resolved to wait until I encountered someone in charge and explain my situation to them.

I could smell the sea. The group slowed their crazy march. I gasped when I saw two enormous wooden ships with masts and rigging. Men were swarming all over the dockside, barrels were being rolled up a gang plank. One of the group dropped me. I hit the cobbles. Then he must have tripped as I felt him land heavily across my back.

'That'll do. Get yerselves over here to declare yerselves,' a voice boomed.

They scurried to form a disorderly queue at an upturned barrel. There a man sat processing men or goods. I tried to speak again, but my voice was drowned out. When we were close enough, I said, 'Sir I just want to explain who I am. I shouldn't be here. I'm not a soldier. I'm not even a man.' He stood up, laughing. 'You're going to have to prove that, me lad.'

I clutched my jacket buttons in terror. This was my worst nightmare.

Yet it wasn't. Just as those around me jerked me backwards, I noticed a sound boom overhead.

Someone shouted 'Cut,' and swore loudly. 'Don't know what happened to the script there, but it wasn't a bad attempt. You made it seem real and that's what I needed.'

Chapter 5- Lost Love

Introduction to Lost Love

This task asked us to construct a story that related to the loss of love in any or its broadest sense, not necessarily the loss of romantic love, and how we perhaps might lose it, be it person or thing, concept or construct. Whether through apathy, carelessness, cruelty, self-sacrifice or squandering, or maturity, there seem to be so many more ways to lose it than to gain it.

Your task might ask you to consider the ways in which love can be lost or gained, whether you choose to do that on a personal level or a more abstract level is up to you. Who lost what and why? Did both people lose it or just one? Was it a permanent or temporary loss? Did it cause pain or sorrow or despair or disgust? Was it purposeful or accidental? You could explore the emotions from the points of view of those that lose it, and the consequences.

If you draw from your own experiences, be cautious, consider if you are ready to explore it, and if you might need some support to do so; or how you might deal with any subsequent emotional fallout. And of course, there is always room for acceptance.

The Ring

Rosemary Blake

Sylvia discovered a Valentine's card in her school locker. Inside it was a ring, hammered out of a ring-pull and decorated with butterflies. Terry caught her eye in assembly and flushed scarlet. After that she was too busy thinking of him to hear the rest of assembly.

So at the end of the day, she waited for Terry by the school gate. He was with a group of lads, but he mooched across to her.

She had been so self-assured in those days. 'Wanna go for a walk?' she'd said. They left the bridlepath and wandered into the woods. 'Thank you for the card.'

He looked down and kicked at the leaf mould. 'S'alright. You knew it was me then?'

She giggled. 'That was obvious. I'd've got one for you if I'd known. You're alright you know, Terry Watson.'

'I think you're alright too, Sylvia,' he said, soppy like. Then he dived forward and gave her a kiss.

It was over fifty years ago. She'd lost the ring, but she could still smell pine needles and feel the rough bark of the tree at her back. She remembered that first brush of his soft lips against hers. If only she could go back. If only their love hadn't been lost.

They had had separate lives. Terry at the factory and Sylvia working part-time as a typist while caring for the family. When the children moved out, nothing changed. Sylvia agreed to help with the grandchildren some days and she'd made a few friends in the neighbourhood. Terry didn't have much to say anymore and he disappeared into his shed.

Once, she put on red lipstick and stood on the threshold. The interior was dark after the sunlight outside, the smells were of creosote, engine oil and wood. Bits and pieces everywhere. How could he work like that? Then he noticed her and frowned. So, she turned and flounced off. If only she had persevered.

But Terry was happy in his shed, she thought fondly. Times, she had had to call and call to get him to come in for a meal and then he'd be itching to get out there again. It used to irritate her. And now it was too late for them to grow closer.

Perhaps, she would be able to feel him with her in the shed. The smell of wood shavings and damp were part of his smell. There were his jars of nails, sets of screwdrivers and the vice sitting as he'd left it. She could imagine him just about to use it. She ran her fingers over the smooth dip in the worn workbench. She opened up his cupboard. In the corner of the shelf, she spotted a tiny wooden box. What had he got there? Inside was the ring-pull ring, looking just as delicate as it had long ago.

Love Lost

P.J. Huckerby

Rusty sills, treacherous brakes and a disinclined second gear couldn't hold back my Austin-Healy Sprite. We'd escape the oppressive city heat of Sheffield… *and her husband* as we sped across the melting tarmac and out to the vast seclusion and romance of the Derbyshire moors. Roof down with a trail of four-star burn in our wake, the two of us would race past scorched lawns and emergency standpipes.

Blonde and volatile, a nineteen-year-old club singer; irresistible in coffee mascara, cherry lips, and semi-perilous platforms. Regalia of leather, crushed velvet and feathers. A distinctive scent: a heady blend of Ambre Solaire, Opium, sweat and Harmony hair spray. She stole my breath.

She captivated me in the summer of seventy-six, bringing a lethal temperature of 96 degrees Fahrenheit and a biblical plague of ladybirds. Those things were beautiful on your hand until they spread their wings…man, they could bite; I suppose more shock than pain.

Dancing Queen on the radio. My untested passion spiralled into raw desire, tropical sunrise, deep blue skies and deep brown eyes. I thought the heat and fervour would surely endure forever. But as the sunrises turned to autumn sunsets and dancing queen yielded to punk rock, first love melted like those Derbyshire roads, and she vanished along with those ladybirds of nineteen-seventy-six.

Love Lost

Cerys Linton

I can still recall my father driving past bomb-damaged terraced houses in London, myself in the back seat, only just big enough to see out of the window of the Cortina. (One of the Mark threes, with the old so-called CND rear lights array, and fins, of all things). This was back in the seventies, but rebuilding was slow. I was fascinated by the insides of the houses exposed to the air, vulgar and naked and sad; the fireplaces, the blackened insides of chimneys, peeling floral wallpaper. I saw a piano still stiffly and formally standing against a wall in an upstairs flat, just hanging there expectantly in space and time, waiting for a nocturne, a polka maybe. I wanted it so desperately to be mine, in that moment.

I remember one Saturday as a child sitting at a piano in our dining room. That piano? It hadn't always been in the family. I found out later that a colleague of my father's was modernising and wanted to dump it, but my father took pity on the walnut veneered beauty. I say colleague, as far as I was aware he had no friends. The piano was one of those old pre-war ideas, that every house should have a piano. But my father was quite modern in his thinking. He put it outside in the rain one day without telling any of us. I had no idea why; maybe it was my playing. It slowly, sadly rotted like the other piano in space and time, and he eventually chopped it to pieces.

But anyway, for now, that Saturday night, the piano still lived. I was plodding through one of my dad's old songbooks, picking out a few notes at a time with excruciating slowness. (He'd been a decent jazz drummer back in the sixties; old photos I have of him are unbearably cool.) I was really struggling with a song called, I think, the *End of the World*. I was probably about seven.

For some reason my mind there and then had a realisation. My father had withdrawn from our world. I was, cliché aside, dead to him, as were all of us. He now existed in a different world. I did not know where this world was. This world did not include me, and I was now irrelevant. The realisation was instant, real, and I understood it was absolutely truthful, and grief expertly carved a hollow in my chest there and then.

There was no acute or inflamed evidence to support this supposition. He behaved as he always did, distant, contemptuous, occasionally angry with us or violent with objects. But he worked very hard and long hours as an executive in a print works. He seemed to be involved in a nightmare of infinite fractalite complexity, as far as my childish mind could tell, and then got home at some point in the evening and instantly hated us. I understood this and why. We were inconsequential at that time but not maybe irrelevant. His apparent contempt and hatred of us made us relevant maybe, and we could still be included in his world at times by this method. He was terrifying in his way, and I wonder now if, as a child, I was actually quite privileged to witness the workings of the mind of someone who truly negates you, but is inextricably bound to you, so the negated one oscillates between non-existence and hated existence.

I remember my odd nightmares of him shouting at us across a vast sea of walnuts while he stood like a god on a piece of furniture he had made. The dream walnuts probably stemmed from a bowl of walnuts on that piece of furniture every Christmas, which always languished ignored 'till my sister and I would hammer the blazes out of them in January to reveal something edible, if withered. The piece of furniture I recently saw on a re-run of the 1960s British TV cult series, *The Prisoner*.

The dead relationship persisted at home for five more years, within my awareness that it was dead and I non-existent and my father a raging cipher. I suppose this is a testament to the resilience of children, and how they still believe in some way that things can work out, somehow resolve into happiness, Enid Blyton style, when they really know it is irretrievable. The realisation came much, much later, that he was an anguished, despairing prisoner in a life he never wanted. He even tried to tell us, if only perhaps through DIY.

He left eventually and married again a number of times, each situation always resolving over time into the same eventual imprisonment of overwork, despair, hatred, unloved children, or being unloved by children. What was he looking for? I always wondered. He found God eventually, but no matter how his faith moved him, I remained in a different, irrelevant world. Perhaps God lived in his world. I hope so.

Cassidy Drums Up Success

Fliss Middleton

Cassidy stares in horror at the blood running down her arm. It hurts, and what is worse, she has done it to herself. She doesn't know what to do about the cuts. The guys on the chatzy site told her she'd feel lifted when she'd done it, but she doesn't, and she's scared.

She begins to shake violently and goes downstairs to show her mum. Mum is shocked and scared too but takes her to hospital straightaway. All the way there, between sobs, Cassidy finally opens about her feelings.

She's broken-hearted that her dad has gone back to America without them and re-married. She's messed about at school and truanted so much she'll probably fail her exams. On top of that, she's been banned from the music studio because of her behaviour. Playing the drums is the one thing Cassidy really loves and when she drums she feels calmer and forgets the negative stuff for a while. She says she feels life isn't worth living and can't see how to make it right. She's sorry to have caused all this trouble for Mum. Mum wants to cry too but has to hold it together to drive.

Within a couple of weeks Cassidy is getting some help from the adults around her. She's been assigned a support worker who has helped her agree a contract with the school about attendance and behaviour in return for studio time.

She gets a video call from Dad which gives her mixed feelings. Just seeing him and hearing his voice brings such a lump to her throat she can hardly speak. He tells her she is going to be a big sister and asks if she would like to come over to the States for her summer holidays this year to see them and get to know her baby brother. Cassidy looks at her Mum who nods and smiles.

Obviously, they have already discussed it. Cassidy is still feeling emotionally fragile. The baby will probably be adorable, but she is jealous too. When Dad pauses for her reaction, she says, 'Thanks Dad but I've got a lot going on right now, I need to think about it and talk to Mum. I'll get back to you.'

He looks disappointed but puts on a brave face. 'Okay honey, whatever is right for you, I'm here for you anytime.' The screen goes blank.

'He didn't even ask me about school, or how my drumming is going,' Cassidy muses later when she's alone in her room. She smiles to herself, 'Actually Dad they are both going great now, your little girl is sure gonna surprise you!'

A few months later Cassidy is called into Mr Pochin, the Headteacher's office. What a surprise Mum is sitting there too! They both look pleased, and Mum looks excited. 'What?' says Cassidy. 'Good News,' says Mr Pochin. 'You've been offered a full-time place at Norton Rock College if you want it? You will continue your education and alongside that will get specialist music tuition to enable you to reach your potential in vocals and the drums. With your Mum's permission, I sent your reports and recordings of your drumming and they have offered you a place for the next academic year. I think you are going to be a star, young lady!!'

That evening at home, Cassidy and Mum celebrate with a pizza and a glass of prosecco. 'I think perhaps I will visit Dad this summer, says Cassidy. 'I need to go before I get too busy and too famous.' They both laugh, then simultaneously choke on the bubbles.

Chapter 6- An introduction to D.A.D.

Within the group we developed a custom of selecting themes or some random objects to inform our writing. The subjects were usually negotiated within the group as they had to lend themselves to a variety of genres.

One subject selected came from a visual prompt brought in by a member. It was a cardboard representation of an open wallet showing paper notes and credit cards. It was designed as a marketing tool and had fallen out of a newspaper.

It was agreed that everyone would endeavour to write a story or poem based on finding a lost wallet or purse and the consequences that followed. The contents of a wallet or purse can say a lot about the owner and there is often a captivating back story to how the loss occurred.

This is where the idea for my story about a lost wallet dropped by a missing father with Alzheimer's came from. I called it DAD after the initials originally embossed on the wallet.

D.A.D.

Fliss Middleton

We found your wallet about a week after you disappeared. It was lying in the mud, to the side of a path, leading into the forest. We knew it was yours as soon as we saw it – a battered old brown leather wallet with your initials embossed in gold, though barely visible after all these years. D.A.D. We used to tease you so much Dad, that your initials were D.A.D. Derek Arthur Davis. I bought you that wallet for your 60th birthday and now you are 82.

I picked up your wallet with trembling hands. I could hardly see through my tears and I knew my sister was crying too though I didn't look at her, afraid of breaking down completely here in this deserted place with my biggest fears overwhelming me.

The wallet felt sodden and slimy with rainfall. Inside a few coins and notes, the notes completely soaked and welded together. Not much else, you didn't need much else Dad -your library card, bank card, bus pass and your discount DIY card. It was this that made me finally succumb to the hopeless overwhelming grief I couldn't keep in. I reached for my sister and we howled like children into the empty tree-lined path.

All the memories came back of you in your garage, your clothes streaked with paint, or sprinkled with sawdust, mending things, making things, the pride you always felt in a job well done. The way you showed your love to Mum, not with romantic gestures, that wasn't your style, but making nice things for the house and keeping everywhere decorated and the garden neat and tidy.

I must have called our uncle because he appeared and was red-eyed but calm and business-like. He phoned the police and they said they would bring officers down to search.

We drove back slowly and sadly to break the news to Mum and to stay with her to wait for confirmation of the inevitable, which we would face together, just as you would want us to, Dad.

Being Herbert

Terri Eynon

'What happened to it, then?'

'To what?'

'The last shift.'

Tom was sure he'd explained that already. He could just about recite the words in his sleep. 'The shortest shift I ever did was my last', Herbert Blake was on record as saying, back in 1992. Thirty years ago now. Tom looked at the woman carefully. Mid-forties, straggly hair streaked with grey, old enough to be Herbert's daughter, he thought. Unmade-up with eyes puffy, as if she'd spent the last two days in tears. Tom had the feeling that, somewhere along the line, he was missing the point. Should he come out of role, say something comforting, he wondered, or just carry on, here in the tally-room, just off the lamp-room, being Herbert Blake. It was something he'd discussed quite often, with the other volunteers. Should you *be* the character or just talk *about* them? He liked to make it real. Like the old miners used to, back in the nineties, when the old Museum was new.

'I went and left home about ten minutes to ten at night and by a quarter to eleven I was back home',' he repeated. One of the group, a bearded man at the back, stifled a yawn. An elderly couple looked at each other, eyebrows raised. 'I came here, took my tally out, said cheerio to everybody and went home. It went back to the days before nationalisation. When anybody retired the manager used to say, 'They don't work on their last shift'. He couldn't bear to have a man killed on his last day at work'.'

‘No, I know all that. My Dad said the same,’ the sad-faced woman chipped in. ‘My Dad worked here until ’86. Only 47, he was, when it closed. They paid him off and he bought a bungalow down Hugglescote. Went into haulage until he retired. No, what I want to know is, what happened to the last shift?’

‘It’s alright Mum, I still remember it.’ The young woman next to her, who also looked rather smudged and tired, took the sad woman’s arm and looked around at the other visitors protectively. ‘I know what she means.’

The elderly couple looked at each other again, this time frowning a little and also smiling, as if recognising something. Something that mattered. Something loved and lost and almost forgotten. ‘You’re too young, my lad,’ said the man, looking at Tom.

‘An incomer, probably,’ the woman replied, as if that explained it.

Tom’s cheeks began to tingle. Whatever an ‘incomer’ was, it didn’t feel welcome. It was all very well learning the Co’ville talk, but he’d never been a miner. Nor his Dad neither. This heritage wasn’t his own.

‘She means *The Last Shift*,’ the young woman said, pronouncing the words slowly and loudly, as if speaking to a foreigner or a child. ‘It stood in the entrance to the old Museum. You know, the one they demolished. When we still lived here, when I was little, we used to come every week. I used to like to ride on the skeleton bikes. In the summer, there was a water-garden with toy boats in wooden canals and all kinds of pumps, like an Archimedes screw and an—’

‘You used to talk to them all, do you remember?’ her mother interrupted. ‘On our way in you’d say, ‘Hello’ and on our way home you’d wave and say, ‘See you next week’. You even had names for them all. Do you remember?’

It was the young woman's turn to go pink. 'Oh Mum!'

'Grandad's friends, you called them,' she said, smiling sadly at her daughter before looking around at the other visitors. 'I was at school when we sculpted them. Four miners back-to-back. Like they were going down the shaft in a cage. All carved out of Ibstock brick.'

'Like they had each other's backs,' said the bearded man, who seemed to have woken up. 'And I know where it's gone. Machine Movers shifted a lot of the stuff. It went back to King Ed. It was still there when my son left school'.

'Can we go and see it, Mum? Grandad would have liked that.'

'If we have time. After the memorial,' her mother replied. 'I'll ring up the school. I expect they won't mind.'

Chapter 7-In the Style of Raymond Chandler

Bourbon on ice

Douglas Gilmour

I put the glass of bourbon down, having two fingers splinted together making it hard not to spill anything. Under the desk lamp I watched blood swirl around the ice, dark in the amber liquid. My tongue searched around my mouth and found the soft socket, where my tooth used to be. I have had better days.

'Well, I hope it was worth it Toto.'

The dog had the good grace to look ashamed as it shuffled round the bed I'd made out of my trench coat. I tossed it another biscuit, but my ribs objected to the sudden exertion. I think I might have passed out at that point, as I missed her coming in. She was silhouetted by the standard lamp in the corner. It was a shape men would kill for, but I had already come close enough to dying tonight. The .38 held casually in her hand was a useful reminder that quite a few had.

'You found Toto, Mr Strachan. Thank you.'

'And in one piece, Betty. The Ant Hill Mob had heard that he must have swallowed the diamonds and were about to try their hand at some do-it-yourself veterinary procedures.'

'Say, I put that story about to buy more time. I was sure whoever had him would wait for things to. . .you know, turn up. I hadn't realised people would be so impatient.' She knelt and stroked

Toto, no mean feat in that dress. The heavy revolver pulled her other hand down so her wrist was open on her knee.

'That story nearly turned Toto into spare parts and me with him. But I guess me and the little fella played our role.'

Betty was scratching through the dense fur around the dog's neck. The terrier rolled over in appreciation. There was still a part of me that would have traded places with the mutt. She glanced up through thick eyelashes, her pupils large with the light behind her. She wasn't giving anything away.

'You look in a bad way Mr Strachan. Does it hurt?'

'Only when I laugh.' I drank from the glass, sieving the ice with my remaining teeth. The whisky stung the inside of my mouth. 'So I should be fine.'

'I'm sorry for your trouble Mr Strachan. I'll write you a cheque. Two hundred dollars as agreed?'

'That would be just peachy.'

'Do you have his collar? And then we will be on our way.' Betty's quick eyes were scanning the room for the padded leather strap. She spotted where I had kicked it, under the dresser. Retrieving it faster than I could think, she ran her hands along the length as she fastened the collar round the dog's neck. She placed the gun on my desk and started fishing through her bag, quickly pulling out a chequebook and a fine, slim, silver pen, long enough to reach a man's heart. Signed with a flourish, gun, pen and chequebook were gathered up. Betty and the dog paused by the door.

'We are both indebted to you Mr Strachan.'

I tried to wave her thanks away but my body wasn't up to that level of exertion and I could only wince as she closed the door behind her. I listened to the sharp heels going down the hall and thought about the swell pins they swung on. But not for long.

I rolled out of the chair and used it to haul myself to my feet. At this time of night, I reckoned it would be forty minutes before she'd made her way across L.A. to her apartment. Thirty seconds to find the gravel I had put in the collar to replace the diamonds and then maybe half an hour back here again. Of course, if she checked in the cab then I was already dead. I felt a little sad at the thought of never laying eyes on that girl again. I held up the glass with the last of the Bourbon and ice that would never melt.

'Here's one for the road.'

Micky Two Hats

P.J.Huckerby

I knew I was in love the second she walked into my office.

'So, you're Micky Two Hats,' she said. 'The private dick.'

I said, 'Yes, who's asking.'

After a toss of her red curls, she responded. ‘Rosy, Rosy Muldoon.’

She came in close…too close, dangerously close. I could hardly contain myself. The heady smell of Avon Sweet Honesty had gone off, but its tart scent only made my heart beat faster, faster than a ferret down a rabbit hole. She looked at me through her thick jam jar bifocals. Her eyes were as big as London bus hubcaps.

Her eyes fixed on mine like a guided missile. ‘Can I trust you?' she asked.

I couldn't speak. I knew this girl was trouble. I should have told her to get out there and then, but I couldn't help myself; I was powerless in her company. It was as though my lips were remote, moving unconsciously. 'Yes.' I replied.

'I knew I could,' she said as she fired up an e-cigarette.

I felt like I'd invited a ravenous leopard into my office.

‘I hope I can. You look like a man I can rely on,' she said and tossed her head back again. I could detect she was wearing a wig, and I wondered what beauty lay under that red thatch. She sat opposite me and seductively unpacked a Lidl scotch egg; she knew exactly what she was doing. I could see it in her gorgeous bloodshot eyes, eyes like an autumn sunset. Her chipped false nails tore skilfully through the scotch egg’s cellophane; she was like a neurosurgeon with those talons. When she bit into the crusty breadcrumb shell, it was plain she was a woman who knew her own mind. The smell of hard-boiled egg was potent and powerful, just like her.

'I want you to follow my husband. I want you to tail him,' she announced.

'£45 an hour,' I replied.

'I'll give you £50 if you kill him.' She didn't look like she was kidding.

I said, 'No less than £100 for murder.' I was kidding; she looked thrilled. 'I'll just follow him for now.'

She passed me an envelope. 'Everything's in there, address, car number plate, photo…’ she said. 'I want to know what that bastard's up to. Jimmy can't be trusted, not like you, Micky.' She paused, wiped the scotch egg crumbs from her blood-red lips with her cardigan sleeve, and sucked again on her e-cigarette. 'Why do they call you two hats?' she asked as she exhaled into my face.

'I used to be a firefighter, and then I decided to become a police officer; two hats, see. I don't wear a hat now.'

'You're boring me,' she said and stood up. 'Keep me updated.' And with that, she left, leaving the scotch egg packet on my desk and a trail of caramel vape smoke in her wake. I flung open the sash window and breathed in the rich aroma of beef batter from the street below. I watched as Rosy crossed the road and into Larry's Fish and Chip Emporium. I do like a woman with an appetite. I looked up above Larry's, across grey rooftops with their ugly satellite dish tumours and beyond to the distant tower blocks on the hazy lip of Rotherham. Their high-rise window squares lit patchy colours in the outlying city fog; they seemed so remote, so desolate. The vision of Rosy Muldoon was now resolutely etched in my mind, my core, clear as a crystal. One hit of that woman was like opium to my soul. I guess I'll never get that woman out of my head. When my assignment's over, I wonder would Rosy be over, or would there be something between us more than a cold transaction? I dare not think. I guess I'm a fool ensnared, a condemned victim of my own heart.

Chapter 8 Grace Dieu

Visit to Grace Dieu Priory

One fine evening we forsook our usual cosy corner in the pub and ventured forth, cameras at the ready, to visit the ruins of Grace Dieu Priory located close by. We hoped that a visit to this ancient monument, in its beautiful setting, would gift us with inspiration for our writings.

We knew a little about the history of the priory and most of the group had visited it previously. Now we approached it with a fresh eye and an openness to whatever effect the visit might have on us in terms of creativity.

Grace Dieu Priory dates back to the 13th Century and was originally built to house Augustinian canonesses. William Wordsworth paid a visit and wrote a poem about it in which he described the ruins as 'ivied' and 'forlorn.'

Happily, we did not concur with Wordsworth and did not find it a desolate place. In fact it was the beauty of our surroundings, coloured by the peachy glow of the setting sun, which inspired my contribution *Bring me Shades*.

Bring Me Shades

Fliss Middleton

Bring me shades of green and brown
The call of birds in the canopy
Spongy leaf mould underfoot
Tiny life forms hidden from me

Bring the sunset filtered gold
Ivy shoots that cleave to bark
Rustling in the fallen leaves
Each tiny creature leaves no mark

Leave me here to watch the night fall
See the glide of ghostly wings
Creatures that attend their business
Furry, prickled, timid things

Give me sunrise in the forest

In the morning chorus let me drown

As the sun lights up the treetops

Give me shades of green and brown

As the sun climbs ever higher

Shafts of sunlight pierce the glade

Dazzled by the sunlit tree trunks

Now, I murmur, bring me shades

Chapter 9 Hallowe'en or Possession

This section is of possession/mystery written for the theme of Hallowe'en night. With *The Museum Hallowe'en Party* we have a trusty attendant who gets more than he bargained for when he unintentionally leaves work late on 31st October. There are all the thrills of things going bump in the night but instead of interrupting historical figures and Neanderthals, he is actually startled by beings not of this world.

With *The Chosen One* we have a tale also set at a party on Hallowe'en night. Although there are characters dressed as witches and so forth, this is no tame gathering but a hard core, black magic revel. Can the main character avoid tragedy and escape the worst consequences of such activities? These stories probe into our fascination with the dark side of the force, be it terrifying characters not of this realm or intriguing human drama leading to evil. With the current fascination for the supernatural in an increasingly materialistic world which does not always satisfy us, we all like to dip our toes into the cold waters of horror whilst being able to retreat to the comfort and safety of our armchairs.

The Museum Halloween party

Dumitru Langham

My name is Milo Edward-Geek, living in New York City working at the Metropolitan Museum of Art. Sorcerer and archaeologist piecing together the past for the wizardry world. Working at a museum certainly has some interesting stories and so too was my experience on October 31st. It was a cold wet miserable day.

It was ten o'clock when things started to get weird. I was planning on meeting up with some old university pals whom I hadn't seen in ages, but as always when you're in a rush to do something, the call of nature interrupts. So, I made a stop at the restroom. As I hurried through the corridor pulling on my duffle coat, I didn't realise how creepy the museum was at night, sinister shadows leering at you in the darkness. Finally, when I reached the comfort of the restroom, I started to notice the flickering hall lights. I heard a loud bang. I quickly looked around. Nothing there. I shrugged my shoulders and carried on into my cubicle. Whoa! I am not going to detail what happened next!! Like most of you who have a smart phone, I'm on it every five-minutes checking up on my Fakebook profile while twirling my pen wand, nearly setting fire to the toilet roll. I shivered as though I was sitting in a freezer, then I heard voices followed by what sounded like music thudding from a stereo. What's going on here? The museum doesn't usually have parties. Just then I looked down to see a transparent head poking through the floor.

'What the—!' I yelled, pulling my trousers up in haste.

'Oh sorry,' said the head, 'I am looking for the main gallery. I hear there is a party going on. Sorry I gave you quite the fright, but I've never been to New York City. Have you seen Drac, Lord of the Vampires? On every Hallowe'en night he uses a dragon-shaped chest to open a portal to the undead world so we can catch up.'

'Well,' I began, 'I haven't heard of any party and could you kindly go through another toilet's floor! And let me finish.' Then I noticed that my phone was getting covered in dust as if people were jumping around. I decided to find out what was happening upstairs. I followed the figure. It was getting colder and colder. When I got to the ancient Egypt section it was full of cobwebs.

The DJ deck and speakers were shaped like skulls. I was amazed by what I saw! It was full of the undead doing a thriller zombie dance of which Michael Jackson would be proud. As I walked, trying not to step through or bump into anyone, I thought they were just in fancy dress.

'Hey, watch it, PAL!' shouted an angry skeleton.

'Oh sorry,' I said, trying to make myself heard over thumping music. I knew that they were not folk in fancy dress but real. My main priority was getting out of there! I passed a vampire complaining that he'd lost the Transylvanian! Just then my mobile went off; it was my mate.

'Hey, where are you?' she yelled. 'We've been waiting for hours.'

'Yeah, I am on my way, got held up with work,' I shouted. Part of me wanted to tell them about the monster party. The other part of me would take my secret to the grave!

Chapter 10- Christmas

Twas...

Douglas Gilmour

Twas the night before Christmas in a north facing bedsit in an Edinburgh tenement. Andrew sat despondently on his bed. The four candles struggled to light the small room while the fire failed to even take the chill off the air. His three children were tucked up in one bed while his own lay like a cold grave beside them. He sat looking at the socks the youngest, Isobel, had insisted be hung above the fire despite her father saying that there would be nothing in them in the morning.

There was a thump and a curse and a tiny man in furs bundled out of the fire and on to the bare boards. He righted himself and dusted off his round belly. He looked around the room and laughed.

'Presents expected but none forthcoming,' he stated.

'No,' Andrew replied, not sure if he was awake. 'I have spent all the silver on candles and coal but still the house is so sombre, dark and cold.'

'I usually ask for the first born to fix such problems, the presents are just a distraction,' said the elf with a wink and jumped lightly onto the bed. He looked critically at the pudgy boy breathing through his mouth. 'But I can be flexible. Cold you say? But the fire is hot I can testify to that.' They both looked at the thin drapes flapping in the draught.

‘Yes, no matter how much paper I stuff in the cracks the chill still comes through,’ said Andrew. The little man walked over to the window with an exaggerated casual air.

‘Sometimes the cause is a little less obvious.’ His hand shot up behind the moving curtain and pulled down an icy leg, a shrieking silvery man followed.

‘Release me Nick!’

‘Jack! You should know better than to have your fun tonight!’ Nick chuckled as the pair struggled and the smaller spirit squealed as he tried to escape. Jack’s wriggling became more spasmodic and then stopped. Nick laughed as he tossed the shining doll up into the air and down into the largest sock.

‘Now then, darkness unwarranted? More parents should listen to their children.’ Nick swung one leg round the other and dove under the bed. Two figures came tumbling out; a black shape wrapped around Nick, its edges blurred and smoky. But Nick, chortling, was on top now, his hands around a wispy neck.

‘Brother!’ gasped the sprite before it froze like freshly broken coal and was spun up to the mantelpiece. Nick looked round the room his eyes twinkling. Andrew backed away till he stumbled on his bed.

‘Am I possessed like Legion?’ asked Andrew. Jack jumped onto the quilt beside him and put his tiny hand on Andrew’s breast, the first hand, tiny or not, to be there for an age. Nick listened to the heart’s story and saw in Andrew’s eyes the disillusioned wife leaving her family for a bottle.

‘There is no inner demon so the charm cannot be completed.’ Nick looked almost serious as he took his hand away leaving a cold spot. He stepped to the other bed and brushed the raven hair of the smallest child.

‘Her laughter will light up a room brighter than a hundred candles. Her wit will be more warming than any fire. You will call her Joy.’

‘Iso. . .’ started Andrew

‘Joy,’ insisted Nick, ‘and you may find happiness in her, while she is with you.’ He kissed the girl on the forehead and whispered something in her ear that made Joy snuggle down beside her sister. Nick looked round the brightly lit room and clapped, he gave the cosy fire a withering look and left by the door.

T'was the Night Before Christmas…

Fliss Middleton

Christmas Eve – it was always Tracey's favourite time. The house had been cleaned and the smell of freshly baked mince pies wafted through from the kitchen. Enticing presents were waiting for them under the tree and their gifts to take to the family were wrapped and bagged in the hallway. Garlands of fairy lights twinkled in the hallway and a pine-cone wreath welcomed them at the door. All that was left to be done was to light the fire, pour a glass of something, open some chocolates and settle back with the TV guide and remote control. Blissful!

Except she wasn't quite ready to relax and sink into the bliss – her husband Paul was out walking their dog, Jarvis, and they'd been gone for ages. She felt a small niggling sense of fear which made her walk out to the front gate and scan the street up and down searching for Paul's familiar walk and Jarvis's reflective collar. No sign of them.

It was the perfect Christmas Eve weather really, a sharp frost had given everywhere a silvery sparkling coating and glancing up into the night sky, she saw that the moon and stars looked brighter than usual and the light from them combined with the frost had a strangely magical effect. But it was cold and she, dressed in her indoor clothes and slippers, began to shiver and hurried back indoors to the warmth.

Her mobile rang. She didn't recognise the number so guessed what might be coming next. Trying not to let her anxiety about Paul, or disappointment at her potentially ruined Christmas Eve, show in her voice, she asked 'What do you need? How many are in the family?' She took a pen and a pad kept for the purpose and began to make a list. Then she wrote down the address and said, ‘Don’t worry I have what you need and will be with you in about fifteen minutes’.

She went to the shelves in the cold outhouse and took tins and packets down, opened the freezer and found meat and vegetables, then added in a couple of selection boxes and some milk from the fridge. She left a scribbled note for Paul near the kettle and got into her car.

The address itself was quite easy to find using her phone but the flat number she’d been given wasn’t so obvious. After a bit of a fruitless search, she had to call the mobile number still on her phone. When the phone was answered it sounded like there was a party going on in the background, which was strange and not consistent with the story she had been given.

‘Please come up, I’m on the first floor,’ said the woman and the door buzzer sounded for her to enter. Reluctantly and wearily, she climbed the dimly lit stairs lugging the carrier bags of food with her.

She knocked on the door and it was flung open by her grinning friend Joy, who pulled her into a raucous cacophony of blowers and party poppers and shouts of ‘Surprise!’ Her eyes went wide at the sight of Paul with a can of beer in his hand and then she spotted Jarvis, the cocker, disappearing under the table with a large sausage roll.

Some ‘so-called friends’ took selfies with her, perfectly capturing her stupid confused grin.

‘So, no-one needs food then?’ she asked rather pointlessly, glancing towards the laden buffet table.

‘Not tonight sweetheart,’ said Paul kissing her cheek.

‘We wanted to throw you a party to say thanks for everything you do,’ said Joy.

‘But I hate parties,’ she laughed.

‘Shut up and dance,’ said Paul smiling and passing her a large glass of something very fizzy.

‘Happy Christmas,’ were the last words she heard before someone turned the music up way too loud.

The Midnight Freight Train

Dumitru Langham

The story that I am going to tell you starts with a neglected old fork track railroad station in Hamilton, Ohio which had been abandoned since the late 70s. A once fine station now fallen into disrepair, the only passengers travelling through the station now are the mice, rats, raccoons and occasional homeless person taking shelter from the weather; and of course, there are the trains themselves, the beating heart of an industry that built America.

Tonight, Christmas, it is dark, cold, foggy, and deep in snow. For Sam, a 16-year-old, it all seemed like a blur to him like the swirling snow. He was wearing oversized hip-hop clothing as he walked towards the station.

He pulled up his oversized brown and golden crown hoodie to hide his white hair and his face. Full of anger and grief, for Sam this was going to be his first Christmas without mum and right now he was also angry at his idiot dad! The thought of his dad brought him shaking with a fresh wave of anger and grief as he leant against the boarded-up graffiti wall that he and his pal did two nights ago.

'Why…why…why did she have to die now!' Sam felt fresh tears welling up in his eyes and wiped them furiously away. The silence deepened; the rumble of traffic faded away, very like his poor mum's life being dimmed out.

As it was Christmas time Sam was listening to Lily Allen's song *Somewhere only we know*, which happened to be his mum's favourite. Sam didn't even move from his spot, apart from spraying swear words about his dad, to join the many on the vandalised door. Then he went back to leaning against the wall. He was the only soul around apart from a scrawny fox which ran out across the track in the hope of finding some food from the trash bin located near a convenience store.

Just then there was a dinging noise as all of a sudden, the railroad crossing bell sounded, and the level crossing barrier was lowered. Sam looked up to see the scrawny fox dart out as though it sensed something approaching. Probably it was an approaching freight train, yet there was no blaring. One sound you can't miss even with your headphones turned to the max, you certainly do not miss the blaring horn of an American freight train. But tonight, there was no such thing, as the eerie silence descended and the fog deepened with fresh flurries of snow which slowly thickened. The station all of a sudden became very sinister. Sam felt shadows leering in the corner. Sam looked up to the rail-crossing bell as it began to swing faster and faster. Sam looked around still expecting to hear the sound of a train horn yet there was none. The rail crossing bell began ringing faster! What the heck is going on, thought Sam. He was starting to feel uneasy. The streetlights began flickering. Sam felt a sudden cold pass over him.

'Remember the midnight horseman.'

Sam about jumped out of his skin; it was the creepy old homeless woman who Sam sometimes saw when he was with his pals. Sam stepped back in horror! Sam fell on the track just as an ear-splitting noise shattered the silent night. Sam looked and to his horror saw in the distance multicoloured lights and heard the deep growling of a huge locomotive. What the heck! Only now a train was approaching! He tried to get up; somehow his laces had got tangled in the track. Panicked he began trying to undo them before the train reached him. Sam looked wildly for the crazy old lady, but she was nowhere to be seen. The frozen track began to shake. Sam looked to see the light of the train getting brighter.

The horns were blasting, but the horn wasn't your traditional horn. It sounded like 'Rudolph the red nosed reindeer.' Abandoning all attempts, Sam knew he was about to be crushed by the massive GE-ac4400cw locomotive. Sam rolled away just in time. When he managed to pick himself up, he saw not one, not two, but four big red locomotives, lit up like a Christmas tree! The lead train had huge reindeer antlers and, on top, a small Christmas tree. The train snaked through town like the Coca-Cola 'holidays are coming' truck, the illusion passing into the night.

Chapter 11- Contradiction

This time our prompt was 'Contradiction'. An abstract prompt like this didn't appeal to many, hence we only have one piece of writing here, but it allows experimentation with genre and meanings or connections. I always begin by consulting a thesaurus. So, Contradiction – paradox, inconsistency.

Ideas to start you off: Can what we see contradict the truth? Science fiction could create a topsy-turvy world.

Why would someone say one thing and then do something contradictory? Perhaps they are frightened of the truth. Being in denial could create a contradiction in their behaviour.

Religious or political fanatics could act hypocritically. If you enjoy writing conflict, the person who contradicts others' points of view could lead to a lively situation. Another way of looking at the concept would be the scapegoat of a family or group who always reacts in a contradictory way.

Try a few rough drafts and see which idea works out best.

A Paradox

Rosemary Blake

Mrs Jones stands at the door to the flat to meet Gillian. Her hair is scraped back into a scrunchie. She wears a bobbly cardigan and terylene trousers. Everything tells Gillian that Mrs Jones has lost hope.

Her tone undermines that impression though. 'There's no need for the whole block to know. Come in, then.'

Gillian tries not to notice the mess. She looks for somewhere to sit. Eyes some papers on the settee and attempts to move them.

'You'll need to find somewhere to sit, but don't move those.'

Instead, Gillian removes a box from a dining chair. She sits with her legs neatly tucked under her and takes out a file from her shoulder bag.

'So, Mrs Jones, your issue is with the tenant downstairs, Miss Anderson.'

Mrs Jones nods, 'She's out at the minute, so you won't be able to talk to her.'

'Okay, have you tried to resolve things with her?'

Mrs Jones pulls in her chin. 'Oh no, you can't expect me to get into a row with someone. It's your job to tell them.'

Gillian purses her lips and says nothing.

'I'm suffering. It makes me so tired. She plays music every night. It's to get at me. I try to make sure she doesn't know where I am, because if she hears me in the bedroom, she'll turn the radio on just below there. So, I have to creep about.'

Gillian notices she does have red-rimmed eyes.

'I see.' It makes Gillian feel heavy. 'What time are we talking about?'

‘Oh, anytime. She wakes me at 4am regular and then again at 6am. It’s ridiculous. If she wakes me early, I try reading and then when she goes out – at about ten o’clock most mornings – I try to get another hour’s sleep.’

‘Maybe she has insomnia?’

Mrs Jones grunts. ‘She clicks the light switch on too. In the night-time quiet I can hear the click. Sometimes she turns ‘er hoover on in the early hours. I know it’s to aggravate me because sometimes she turns on the radio when she isn’t even in the room with it.’

‘I see. Can you think why she might want to bother you?’

‘I ‘spose it started when she first came. She waltzed up with a group of young men to help her move in. Her brothers, her boyfriends, whatever, with boxes and furniture. They were messing about and I could hear her shrieking with laughter. She brought her dachshund and I could hear her shouting, ‘Get outer the way mutt. Shurrup or you won’t know what hit you.’ I could hear it whining and scraping at the door. I can’t bear cruelty to animals. Then I stomped on the floor and shouted, ‘No you shut up.’ I must admit, it was after that, that it all started.’

Gillian examines her nails and lowers her voice to sound sympathetic. ‘I’m afraid there have been reports that you play loud music and sing at odd times too.’

‘Well of course, that’s just bin sometimes when she’s quiet. I think, well, see how she likes it.’

‘Unfortunately, it has an impact on other tenants.’

‘Well, yes it will.’

‘You will be pleased to hear that Miss Anderson is moving out next month. But we should talk about how to avoid neighbourhood problems.’

Mrs Jones stills. Gillian is puzzled by the silence.

Mrs Jones mutters, ‘I don’t know how I feel about that. The hussy’s going? But she’s only just got here.’

‘Well, she found another apartment. So…’ Gillian trails away.

Mrs Jones seems to fold in on herself. ‘I hope I haven’t forced her to move.’ Then she rallies, sitting up straight. ‘And if she just leaves, she’s got away with it. She’s bothered me but you haven’t told her. You people should have come sooner.’

‘Well, you can forget about Miss Anderson now.’

Mrs Jones shakes her head. ‘Hmm, Miss Anderson. Hussy Anderson more like. I wonder where she’s off to. My life’s going to change. It’ll be awfully quiet around here and then how do I know who else is going to move in? I will have to get to know them all over again.’

With a tight smile Gillian says, ‘I’m going to give you a leaflet on how to resolve neighbourhood disputes.’

Chapter 12- Pink

This time our task was to write anything around the colour Pink.

Pink

P. J. Huckerby

'Just thought I'd catch up with you before joining the others in the pub. Mum's not far away; just past those yew trees, just over there, near the wall…see? God, it's cold. Should've brought a coat; I wanted to show off my suit, though. I don't often wear one nowadays. I can't even remember when I last…'

'Now I'm here, I don't really know what to say. I've so much to say, stuff, you know, so much to say, but now I can't think, funny that. Well, anyway, good to talk, you know, without you giving me a lecture.

'Hey, do you remember Eric Armitage? He couldn't make it today; emphysema really bad; no surprise, though, not really. He smoked like my Morris, you remember?

'Every Saturday, you took me to that dingy place; Arkwright Snooker Hall. Stank of beer, fags and piss; God, I hated that place...I was so bored. Don't know why you dragged me off there. Suppose 'cos mum was working, guess you couldn't leave me on my own, I wouldn't have minded. I say I hated the place; it wasn't all bad. I liked the rows of overhead table lights, all ensnaring swirling smoke in their radiant nicotine beams. You could smoke fags indoors then; it was almost compulsory in that bloody place. Eric Armitage; never saw him without a massive bloody cigar in his mouth, only took it out to play a shot or swig his stout. Somehow those snooker balls looked unreal, magical to me then. Like they were from outa-space or something, gliding in the spotlight across the gleaming green baize. My favourite was the pink ball; wow, it really popped; if there was ever a colour that looked like it was from another planet…oh wow.

‘Remember when I got ready for my first job. I was so nervous, so, so scared. I got this tie. I bought it specially. Pink it was, to give me self-assurance. I liked it because it reminded me of the snooker hall; I don't know why. Anyway, you went crazy mocking me, telling me I looked like a…God, you can't say that stuff nowadays…not even sure you could back then. Mum rounded on me as well, both of you mocking, cackling and pointing. Do you remember her cackle? You two were like jackals sometimes. All those critical glances behind my back, rolling eyes and lip curl. You were the worst, never satisfied.

‘You wanted me to work in construction like you, but I bloody hated it; never dared tell you. I couldn't do a thing, anything without hearing your self-righteous tongue, a judgemental barb on anything and everything; my job, my car, my friends, everything, everyone, nothing was good enough. Even when you weren't around, I could see you plain as day, shaking your head. Clothes, friends, and even the way I eat; you'd find a problem.

‘Hey now, don't you worry about mum, she'll be okay enough. She's going to Bright Horizons Care Home. I arranged it last Tuesday. Her memory's shot now anyway, of course, you know that. Look, I know, I know what you're going to say. Bright |Horizons was nearly shut down due to poor hygiene. Oh, that sex scandal and the alleged cruelty; I'm sure it's all blown out of proportion; you know what social media, T.V. and papers are like. I know you love her, worship the ground, but it's for the best, and it's the cheapest, so that's that, it's all arranged now.

‘So here we are, and I thought I'd say, say how I feel, you know, before I go to the pub, join the others. I guess I feel liberated somehow…whatever that means. God, it's cold…that's a chill breeze, north wind. You must hate this suit. I was going to tone it down and get the salmon pink, slightly more subtle, but I thought why, I mean why not, so I got one tailor-made in bright pink, just like that snooker ball. You must loathe it, but that's not all; you'll never guess. I've been to see Larry at the stonemason suppliers. You remember him, I'm sure? Anyway, you know what? They can do a marble in pink. Larry said the colour may be inappropriate for you, a man's man like you who worked in construction, but I insisted. See, I'm getting more assertive nowadays. Anyway, I've decided you should have one with gold lettering on pink marble. I know it's a bit Liberace, but it makes me so bloody happy, and what can you do about it now, Dad? You're facing eternity under a pink headstone.'

Chapter 13- Writing Comedy

Somebody came up with the idea that we should write something deliberately and explicitly funny. I think we all found it one of the hardest challenges of the year. There is something crippling about the instruction 'be funny'.

That said the stories produced a good few laughs on the night. Possibly because we all found it so hard only one has made it to this collection.

The Florist

Douglas Gilmour

The funeral was three days after Christmas. Someone had lit all the decorations which made the crematorium look cosy against the day's thin blue light. Alice sat in the back row, still struggling to find the right words for the eulogy. Uncle William's estranged wife was at the front leaning over the open wicker casket with a bottle of her infamous homemade vodka. Aunt Susan had insisted on the casket being opened just to prove that he really had gone. It seemed to be one slug for her and one for him which William, as a lifelong teetotaller, would hardly have appreciated. She was using lots of words but most of them were slurred and none of them were much use to the writer.

People had started to drift in for the service, but they were hard to spot given the vast array of flowers that filled the space between the pews and the coffin. Alice made a last correction and went forward slowly to her seat. Slowly, as Alice was struggling to see with streaming eyes and nose. Her hay fever was really making the most of this unexpected mid-winter floral bonanza.

'I didn't know Alice was that close to Bill.' The comment drifted through the gathering congregation as they glanced, concerned, at the teary-eyed niece. The words startled the grieving widow who offered one last drink to the departed, tapped the lid shut and hastily stuffed the badly sealed bottle back into her bag. She dragged the clinking hessian holdall back to her seat using various flower stands for support on the way. She sat opposite Alice, a poinsettia and holly arrangement holding a bright candle between them. Alice tried to smile at her aunt but had to blow her nose instead.

The Crematorium was full and the service started. Susan snored gently. Alice's tears were in full flow as she stumbled her way to the lectern, vaguely aware of having knocked the decoration as she stood. Her speech seemed to pass in moments but, despite the snuffling, Alice thought it had all gone rather well.

'So in conclusion. When he found himself accepted by you – the organisation he came to value most – Uncle William found the tranquillity he was looking for. A peace, I think, we have all found reflected here in today's service.' Alice nodded to the verger and the coffin started to slide forward as 'Angela', the theme from *Taxi*, started to play.

There was a pop and a tiny blue shockwave expanded out from Susan's vodka-soaked handbag. Alice watched as the flames leapt across the tiles, a willow-the-wisp version of Usain Bolt. Three of the intervening wreaths went up like roman candles. Alice watched the blue fairy of death dash past her feet and up into Bill's casket. Susan's sharing must have dripped through the wickerwork as the whole thing went up with a 'Whoomph'.

Sprinklers started, triggered by the burning displays. The wooden arch above the furnace protected Will and his gathering conflagration, leaving the ineffective water to pool underneath. It gave the burning coffin the effect of a funeral Viking longship gliding across a lake. Heavy velvet curtains swung together in their symbolic act of closure, but the old gods were not ready to let go of William so easily. Fire zipped up the polyester, scorching fabric free of the supporting rings. Released, the curtains collapsed in a roaring mass around the ship as it travelled to the next world.

The fire formed a giant flaring hand searching the roof for escape. But the doors shuddered shut on Hugglescote's answer to Up Helly Aa, the damaged but implacable cremator mechanism having won its battle with the pagan past.

The sprinklers shut off. Hush fell. A smouldering Woodland Pillow with (burnt) Chrysanthemum Highlights slid into the water with a hiss. Dismissed, the saturated Leicestershire Floral Society stumbled their way towards the exit, stunned into silence by their President's unexpected entrance into Valhalla.

Chapter 14- Outcast

This assignment was set for us to tackle a character set apart from society. To draw the reader in from the start. To place the protagonist in a desolate and hopeless place on the fringe of acceptance. He or she could be a pariah exiled for being immoral, evil, or simply misunderstood. This is an excellent way to create sympathy for a misjudged character or argue the case for your protagonist.

Blonko

Peter Huckerby

Simon remembered. The past was all he had; the present had no need for him now. No one had any time or interest in who or what Simon ever was. He'd become a relic of the last century. He wasn't even a curiosity to them; nobody cared.

Simon had been an alcoholic most of his life. It was a miracle he could remember anything at all, least of all about the glory days. But Simon could remember. The memories were scrappy but bright enough. He held on to those fragmented recollections like a shipwrecked man clinging to driftwood in an indifferent sea.

His flat was six-hundred square feet of clutter, but to Simon, it was a treasure trove of a golden age. That age, however, was not all golden for Simon. He'd been a drunk playing the part of a drunk. A tragic comic, a fool to laugh at. He was as much a prisoner as the performing animals he'd shared his life with all those years ago. After his wife left him, he drank more. The irony was that he was better at his job drunk…funnier.

Now though, Simon shared his life with no one. He was a relic, alone, cast aside.

He looked around his tiny world. The walls adorned with faded posters of acrobats, lions, tigers, performing elephants and his friends. At ninety, he'd outlived his pals and co-workers. He was an alcoholic, yet he'd survived his more athletic peers. At least this granted him a kind of poignant sense of achievement.

Only for ten of his ninety years on earth could Simon honestly claim any shred of happiness. He picked up the headlight of Nelly, the last remains of his performing circus car, and held it to the window to catch the sun. The chrome was tarnished, yellow paint chipped and faded. But to Simon, the portion he held aloft allowed him to visualise the rest. The comedy car, the door falling, wheels adrift, honking the horn and the audience…*oh, oh, the sound of the audience.*

The smell of the sawdust and wet canvas and those roars and applause. Nelly was his prop, the highlight of his act. After all these years, he could taste the atmosphere, the candyfloss, greasepaint and smouldering lights. He remembered the constant generator drone, the glamour and pageantry, and living cheek to jowl with his friends and animals.

The old man looked down through his window at the empty streets. Not a soul to be seen. The deserted town and boarded up shops only reminded him of how his audience had forsaken him.

With the demise of the Big Top in the 1970s, he was pitched against his friends. Thrown into an ever-shrinking employ. His friends became rivals in a diminishing market. All scrabbling for T.V. appearances, walk-on parts, holiday camps and the tragic and desperate children's party circuit. But the clown was no longer fun, no longer a joyful interlude from the high wire and performing beasts. The clown had become the mask of the devil, the face of nightmares.

Now though, nonagenarian Simon was in a high-risk category and confined to his home. In truth, he'd been isolated for decades. He was a man without a purpose marooned in the twenty-first century. Not a glance in his direction, everyone's eyes are now immersed in the synthetic reality of flat screens, filtered teenage influencers, Instagram and TikTok. Yet as the virus struck fear across the globe, a clown's face was not so much the focus of fear as it was.

Simon sat across from the dressing room mirror he stole all those years ago, his reflection encircled by twelve dead lightbulbs. He tapped one into life and began. He smeared the greasepaint gently. Meticulously applied with frail fingers and brush until Simon faded away and Blonko the Clown returned for one last time. The dry cough and sweat were the tell-tale signs. The old man was a smoker and alcoholic with diabetes and athlete's foot. He was no buffoon now, though; he knew his final curtain call was upon him as he applied a dignified final touch…the red nose. A classic and tragic fool.

Chapter 15-An Unexpected Happening

The Supermarket

Fliss Middleton

She cou ld remember most of the details of the robbery which turned into a murder. She kept replaying it like a peculiar film in her head, sometimes speeded up, at other times in slow motion. People running, shouts, the sound of gun shots, screams and blood running like a little river under the trolleys in the trolley park. This film played day and night in her head so that she could barely eat or sleep.

A week on and the police tape had been removed, but she was sure she could still make out the outline they drew around the shape of the poor young manager. And the bloodstains were there too…but was she just imagining that? She tried not to think about the blood, but her eyes kept going back staring in fascinated horror. She was sure she could still see these details even though the area was covered with wilting flowers and burned-out tea-lights now.

It had been just a normal day at the supermarket, picking up a few bits for her tea and food for the cats. The aisles were busy, people chatting, babies crying, trolleys being wheeled stiffly around, tills opening and closing and the smell of fried bacon wafting out from the café.

Then strange things began to happen, although people seemed to carry on what they were doing for ages, as if they couldn't comprehend the sudden change to their well-established routines.

She saw the manager sprinting towards the cigarette tills and heard him yelling at the men who were grabbing the packets and the lottery tickets and hitting the tills with metal bars and threatening the frightened assistants. People were shouting and pointing. Alarms were sounding and suddenly the men turned and ran out of the store. The manager ran after them – she didn't know why. Why not just let them go?

He probably didn't think it through, was full of adrenaline and didn't see the gun till it was too late. There was a shot and one scream quickly followed by the sounds of a car revving up and driving off with squealing tyres. Just like in the police programmes.

Police and paramedics showed up in vehicles with blue flashing lights and got everyone out of the store and away. She somehow made it home, although hours passed before she realised she hadn't taken off her coat or fed the cats.

She heard they were going to organise a fun day to raise money for the manager's family. She would probably go to support it although she wasn't much for fun these days and she wasn't sure it was the right kind of event to honour a 'Have-a-go-Hero' as they called him in the newspaper.

She thought a bench would be a more fitting tribute. Somewhere the older folk could rest their legs and put down their bags-for-life for a while. Maybe someone would sit down for a chat and she could ask them if they were still as scared as she was, and if they too watched it like a film over and over again.

Chapter 16- First Chapters of Our Novels

And so, from using random words to write a story, to those of us who decided to write a whole book.

Peter, our founding member, first published a non-fiction book in 2015. A multi-talented artist, we are grateful to him for our fabulous cover design. Douglas and Rosemary's books are already available to buy and I am hoping to make mine available in 2023.

Exciting choices about what genre to write in and whether to pursue a professional career. Now it's over to you to decide…

Enjoy

Macy xxx

If you want to continue reading:

Rocket Surgery by Douglas Gilmour enter amzn.to/3P3At6G into your web address bar

Rosy's Recycling Tea Shop by Rosemary Blake, enter amzn.to/36PUego into your web address bar

New Year Newish Me by Macy Milldale- watch this space in 2023..

Easy Visual Merchandising by Peter Huckerby enter amzn.to/37s16Bu

From **New Year Newish Me**

Macy Milldale

‘How do I look in this?’ Claire tottered around the changing room, striking different poses as if on the catwalk.

Dee smiled wryly at her friend’s daring exhibition in front of the teenage girls in the communal area.

‘Go on Dee, go get that little red number to try on. I know you think it will clash with your hair, but it won’t. Try something different for a change other than black.’

Not wanting to disappoint her friend Dee launched herself back into the hell hole of a shop that was known to cater for adolescents. She wandered aimlessly unable to recollect where the dress was. She would try it on to amuse her friend but had no intention to buy it.

The jangle of the music and the brightness of the lights made her feel a little light -headed. She was not feeling the spirit of the annual Christmas party dress hunt.

Dee was distracted by the snippets of conversations she heard while scanning the aisles. She was also bemused by the display of selfies being taken by girls who were sending photos of the items they were considering buying and waiting back for snapchat approval from besties. She was of course feeling envious, that she was not at a stage in her life when all that was at stake was whether to go vampy or geeky. She was thirty-five, after all.

The scarlet dress was glittering in the corner of the shop. It called to her. Dee stood transfixed and dreaming of having the kind of figure that would show it off. It was of course designed for a waif with pert breasts. It would also be a disaster to wash, as it had sequins on and she needed to think practically. She grabbed it as if it were a lifejacket under a plane seat and scurried off to the changing room.

Back in the cubicle she reluctantly unzipped her jeans and pulled off her jumper. It was so cold as well and the lighting was so unflattering. If she could just breath in a little more she could ease it over her hips without splitting the seams. Alas, the zip at the back just would not do up and she stopped the contortionist act.

'Now my mascara has run and I look like Alice Cooper,' she thought to herself. She didn't know whether to laugh or cry.

Claire was trying on a bodycon for her winter getaway. She looked at her shapely, toned body in the mirror. She avoided looking at her inner thigh but had to concede in the end.

'Damn, I'll have to wear a long skirt.' She ripped the dress off and slung it at the hanger.

'How you getting on with that dress Dee?'

'No good, I couldn't get it on.'

'Are you sure?'

'Come and see if you don't believe me.'

Claire ripped open Dee's curtain and looked her friend up and down.

‘Come on let’s go for a coffee. I’m sure you will find something online.’

The two friends walked arm in arm, the same way they had done since when they first met at nursing college. There was not long as it was nearly closing time at the shopping centre. People were scuttling by, rushing to catch the bus and to get home for hot tea after a stressful evening of Xmas shopping. All were laden with bags of toiletries and other items that would end up in tombola raffles later in the year. The aroma of the coffee shop beckoned them in and it felt like a welcome retreat.

‘There you go, lemon drizzle.’ Claire knew that cake always cheered her friend up.

‘Will you have half with me?’ Dee knew that her friend would always refuse.

‘Come on then Dee. New Year and all that, are you going to look for another job?’

‘Yeah and get a new man and lose half my body weight.’ She said this in between negotiating mouthfuls of a particularly dry slice of cake.

‘What about you then Claire? You said you wanted to travel more and take up yoga.’

‘I never plan anything you know that.’ She was a little distracted by a business type with a sharp beard, who was scrolling on his phone.

‘Are you ready for another relationship do you think? It’s been a while and you said you were fed up with being on your own.’

‘Maybe, if not I might go to the Amazon and study the wildlife. Hopefully there’ll be some Tom Hardy look-alike working there as an anthropologist.’ She giggled and then suggested it was time for them to go.

Dee drove home, the rain pounded down and the glare from headlights made her eyes feel heavy. She hoped her mum was still up, ready to make her a hot chocolate and to have a chat or maybe watch some television.

Dee thought about her life. She wondered if she would ever feel completely happy.

She thought for a moment whether it was possible to have a life like those in the TV realities shows ‘The Housewives of Timbuktu?’ Surely it was all made up and anyway she would not want to just party all day. She also disliked false nails. She remembered how she had once paid forty pounds for a set before going on holiday, she lost one doing her suitcase zip up and a further one somewhere on the plane. She recalled how it had worried her immensely as she never tracked it down and wondered if it had ended up in someone’s microwaved dinner.

The stupid satnav, for some reason when she was tired, or it was dark, all the roads look different and now she was heading the wrong way on the motorway.

She started to think about the self-esteem group and what and how she wanted to change in the New Year. At fourteen stones, she knew she needed to lose weight, not just for her body image but also her health.

She pictured her body. She had nurse’s legs, heavy and blighted by broken capillaries. She had nurse’s arms, muscular but thick. Somehow or other she had ended up though with a sumo wrestler stomach and bum, which was of course nothing to do with nursing. She reminded herself she had not watched

'Embarrassing Bodies on catch-up yet. She felt down in the glove compartment and how lucky it was that a chocolate twirl was still left over from the multi-pack. She was feeling a little hungry.

Dee's mum was still up but her dad had gone for his Friday drink. She was watching a recorded episode of 'Vera' but paused it to speak to her daughter.

'Shall I do us a drink love?'

Dee slumped in the armchair nearest the fire. She looked up at the bookshelf and her school photo when she was four. It had taken pride of place there since she had started school alongside a photo of her when she had qualified as a nurse. Claire was also on the photo as Dee's mum had felt sorry that Claire's own mum had not attended the graduation ceremony.

'Do you want a bit of that cherry cake from yesterday love?' her mum shouted from the kitchen.

'Thanks Mum.'

'So how was our Claire then?'

'Still spending too much money on clothes and avoiding having a relationship. Other than that, okay.'

'I don't understand her. Looking how she does, being a matron and owning her own house. You think she would want a family by now.'

Dee shot a glance at her mum. Her mum noticed it and avoided eye contact with her daughter.

‘I don’t think Claire’s interested in being a mother. What you’re really trying to say is that I should have a home and family.’ Dee gazed at the dying embers of the fire.

‘It wasn’t a dig at you love. You’ve just got to be careful who you fall for next time.’

‘Well, we thought that Martin was decent to start with.’

‘He was just obsessed with that son of his. Was it three times a week he was taking him to rugby? He never made any time for you.’

‘I know and then there was Luke before him. If only he had carried on with his gambling counselling we may have made it work.’

‘This year you will meet someone Dee, you can’t be unlucky forever.’

‘Yeah, maybe Mum.’

After eating the cake, Dee was struggling to keep her eyes open and so she retired to her bedroom. Good old mum, she had put a hot water bottle in her bed, and she snuggled deep under the duvet.

The last thought she had before nodding off, was a reminder to buy a lotto ticket as it was a roll over and she could change so many people’s lives with it. She could pay for a psychologist for Claire to see why she was afraid of relationships, then she could treat herself to an elephant sanctuary as well as a thatched cottage with a climbing rose. She then started to worry about how she could accommodate an elephant sanctuary in the Cotswolds. Perhaps she could just fund one in Africa and have a webcam instead?

Claire meanwhile was tossing and turning as usual. She grabbed a magazine and irritably flicked through the pages. Maybe Dee had been right about trying a relationship? She could also go to the self-esteem group with her, just to support her. She wouldn't get any benefit from it herself. The curtains were allowing a sliver of light through and there on the bedside table was the knife.

From **Rosy's Recycling Tea Shop**

Rosemary Blake

'No don't go in.' Rosy's mother burst out of the church, her hands clenched into fists.

Rosy faltered. She felt her father's arm tense, clamping her to him, but she was still stepping forward focusing on reaching the church doors. The headdress pulled on her hair roots as Tanya, holding the veil, failed to keep up. Rosy broke free from her father's grasp and charged towards the entrance.

'No stop.' Her mother darted after her.

Rosy went through the church porch to open the inner door. Some guests were rising from pews and gathering belongings. Several turned curiously to look her way. No one stood at the altar – so Jack hadn't arrived. Her mother grabbed her elbow.

'I'm so sorry. He said he couldn't go through with it,' she said.

Rosy spun around. 'What? Did he say that to you?'

'Yes, he was here very briefly. I had no idea what was going on. Then he left.'

'Did you ask him why?' Rosy couldn't breathe.

'Come on.' Her father laid his palms on both of their backs. He suddenly looked old. 'Joan, you take Rosy back to the hotel. I'll go in and speak to the guests.'

Rosy fled along the walkway back to the hotel. She was hampered by her mother clinging to her arm. Rosy wanted to run, but not just to the room where moments ago she had been excitedly getting ready.

Without halting, she asked, 'Is Jack alright? Where did he say he was going? I just need to speak to him.'

The staff behind the hotel reception looked startled, but she just marched past. In the bedroom, bridesmaid Tanya tried to help. She reached out for Rosy, but that was no comfort.

Rosy plucked at the frothy white layers of her dress. 'I need to get away from all this.' She ripped the veil from her mop of curls. The dress lay on the carpet like a collapsing meringue.

She caught Tanya's arm. 'I can't stay here. I can't face the guests. I need to get home. Will you come with me?'

Her mother, Joan sat on the bed. 'Do you want us to come down to Somerset? I don't like to think of you on your own. We could come just for the next few weeks?'

'No, your flights back to Spain are booked. I know you need to get back. At least I'll feel at home in Somerset and anyway Tanya will be with me.'

Joan wrung her hands, 'I suppose so. And you've got Stella. She's not far away and she would pop around. She's a good sort.'

Rosy nodded. When she was small, the family had lived in Somerset and Stella had been their teenage babysitter. Later the family moved away for Rosy's father's job.

Tanya had changed out of her bridesmaid dress and said, 'But what about you and Jack?'

Rosy shook her head as though trying to dislodge an annoying fly. Somerset was also where Rosy and her fiancé Jack had returned to build up their business. No doubt Jack would turn up there too. Since she had settled there with Jack dear old Stella had become nothing but a busybody, but oh well, it made her mother feel more comfortable to think that Stella would help.

As much to reassure her mother as to answer Tanya, she said, 'I'll be fine. I don't know whether Jack's going to go back home too. I hope he doesn't think he's going to walk in there without answering a lot of questions.' She couldn't turn off her feelings for him, but at the same time her hurt felt like a gnawing stomach-ache. 'I'm sure I'll feel better as soon as I'm away from here.'

Joan hesitated, looking unconvinced, but at that moment Rosy's father arrived and offered to carry the bags to the car.

Once on the road, Rosy stayed silent. She couldn't process anything. They were driving into the setting sun so it was irritating when it shone below the sun visors. The tarmac was still slick from an earlier shower, so Tanya probably thought that she was concentrating on the road. Questions were racing through her mind. How long had Jack been having doubts? Was anyone else involved? Had he ever loved her?

Eventually she exploded with words. 'There must be someone else involved. But who? He'd seemed to be okay, hadn't he, when you saw him? It makes you wonder – did he ever really love me?'

Tanya said, 'He was always chilled. Of course, he must have loved you.'

Rosy barely heard Tanya's soothing tones. 'We were supposed to be flying out to Turkey this evening. We needed that holiday. We'd paid for a balcony with sea view. All the money we spent. I don't suppose we'll get a refund.' Rosy shook her head. 'And the plans for the old bakery – all that time spent renovating it. He's ruined it. I can't see how we can launch the tea shop now.'

'I know hun, all your dreams for a future. I didn't get to see you much in the last few months. Maybe all that work and the wedding got to you both? Perhaps he'll come to his senses now the pressure's off,' Tanya said.

'He'd have to have an exceptionally good excuse for this. No there couldn't be an excuse good enough. I could never trust him again. He didn't even stay to explain.'

They stopped at traffic lights in the centre of a small town. 'What about our money?' Rosy said quietly, her fingers drumming on the steering wheel. 'I'll need to speak to the bank. I'll show him. I can make a go of it on my own,' Rosy said, 'well I have to.' It was said defiantly, yet being without him was like losing one of her arms.

As they reached the countryside she loved, Rosy stared out at the now darkening hedges occasionally lit up by her headlights. She and Tanya tried to imagine the conversation at the reception after they had gone. She felt awful that her parents had had to face everyone and deal with the hotel. It had taken them years to get over the death of her brother Alex, and now this. Once her father retired, they'd moved to Spain and built a new life. Rosy was afraid that her situation would cause them anguish all over again.

She tried to focus inwards for a moment. If she couldn't summon all of her positivity, she was scared that she'd sink. She needed to pull it together again so that she could put on a brave face for the people who knew them in the village.

From **Rocket Surgery, Chapter One**

DJ Gilmour

Ben takes another swig from the pint of water on the shelf in the hall. It is his fifth and his stomach is beginning to hurt. 'I'm too sexy for my shirt' drifts in from the kitchen with the first of the morning sunshine. Ben camps it up to the mirror, he back-combes his long, thin, blonde hair and mouths 'lovely' to himself. His reflection flutters its eyelashes in appreciation. Ben smooths his white T-shirt and stands by the door. A sealed packet of Benson and Hedges slides into its usual pocket, keys into the other. Another half-empty packet is propped up by the folded back lid. Ten filters, still in their perfect three deep formation, peek out at him. He pulls one out, lights it and takes a final big swig.

'Drinks too wet without one.'

The lighter drops into the pouch already marked out for it in stressed denim, 'Five pints of water without going for a slash,' the smoke billows out of his mouth as he talks. 'Gotta be a record,' he looks round the flat with only a single chair in the centre of a bare room and tugs the door to.

The sun still has that clean look of an early morning in Slough. Later it starts to look red and uncomfortable as all of the pollutants (physical and spiritual) below begin to knock out its earlier optimism. It will be a saddened and world-weary star by the time it sets, dark in an orange sky above the Thames Valley.

Now, though, it is beautiful- just as he had been at the start of things. The six starlings that constitute the wildlife of the street are deep in conversation as Ben bounces down the steps. This is their moment when they can catch up on the news without shouting. In another hour Windsor Road will be fulfilling its function as a car park extension from Windsor to Slough. The M4 at the end of the street is already supplying the backing track of roaring tyres, while the forty-five second cycle at Heathrow and the fast trains to Paddington take it in turns to raise the sound level just beyond the level of tolerable.

Ben, though, is oblivious to all of this; he has been here too long. Returning from his travels around the UK it is everywhere else that is really quiet. He stoops to check the laces of his fourteen hole Doctor Martin boots in traditional black. Ox blood red would be better but he hasn't had the spare cash for a long, long time. He breaths in deeply, spreading his arms wide. He can feel the mass of water moving uneasily in his stomach. Ben has memorised the route. It takes about thirty minutes in the car, at an average say of twenty miles an hour, so ten miles. It is no longer than walking to Glen Fruin and flatter, so it shouldn't be a problem.

Ben remembers climbing over the Hill to Glen Fruin. The Hill doesn't have a name. As children they had checked on a dozen maps to see if they could find out what it was. In a land where every ridge and rock manages a name of a budding Rob Roy extra, the two thousand five hundred foot mountain that separates the Fruin and the Clyde remains the Hill with No Name. Ben wonders what is the hill equivalent of a cigar and poncho? From the top of the Hill you can see north to Ben Lomond, west to the Arrochar Alps and east to the Gargunnock hills. To the South, beyond the sparkling Clyde and the Sugar Boat stands Goat Fell on Arran and the Paps of Jura. Thoughts of the Paps of Jura reminds Ben of Clorinda.

Clorinda Ferguson. Red hair, the tightest of jeans, a chest that deserved a mapping expedition all of its own. Released early from his Aunt's shop, Ben and Clorinda had climbed the Hill and only then thought of Craig's Pool. The pool was where the Fruin Burn deepened and slowed for a while on its way through the highlands to the sea. The water, ice cold despite the heatwave, always posed a tricky problem. Stay below the water as much as possible and experience the first stages of cryogenic freezing. Stay above the water and the vicious Argyll Cleg would strip the flesh from an exposed limb in seconds. Or at least give you a nasty nip. No costumes? No problem, they stripped off and dived in. The prospect of snogging Clorinda provided a brilliant solution to the bitter cold. Her body stretched the surface tension of the still pool, rolling onto her back and gliding to the gravel of the far bank. Ben, teeth flashing, slid after her, only his eyes above the surface, the Jaws theme running in his head.

A squeal of dusty breaks made them both turn in the water. A yellow Escort Mexico pulled up at the car park about a hundred yards from the pool. A short, fat man in a brown shirt rolled out with four kids boiling out behind him. Something frightening rocked the car as it shifted out of the passenger side. Ben straightened slightly to get a better look, it must have been female once, but there could be two, maybe three of Clorinda there. Ben looked back at the man scratching the underside of his gut and stretching. The dark circles in the nylon shirt took the scent out of the heather from here. Behind him Clorinda swore.

'Aye. Frightening what can happen if you don't take care of yourself. Nice car though.'

'Eh? The clothes you bloody idiot!' Ben started towards the pile but he realised that despite contact with the wintry water, he was charging towards four kids with his tackle stiff enough to double as a towel rail. The children looked rather taken aback, as did the nylon-clad driver.

‘Hey. You. What the hell do you think yer doin?’

‘I. It’s not. Shit!’ Ben gathered all that he could from the shore and splashed back across the river. About two thirds of the way across he had to swim. One armed but fast, as the lumbering Ford owner closed. Clorinda was shouting abuse equally at both men from the dangerous shelter of a gorse bush. Ben hauled himself up the bank and kept on running across the grass and heather to the yellow flowered spiky cover. The pair pulled the wet clothes into two piles as the man stood up to his not inconsiderable waist in the water inviting Ben to pop back for a chat. With the gorse to their backs they dragged on what they could and squelched up the hill. They were still laughing when they reached the top. Holding hands as they looked out over Argyll. She hung her bra on a battered rowan, followed by Ben's shirt. He stretched, conscious of his easy muscularity.

I looked fine and dandy in those days, fine and dandy. Had it all then, Ben thinks as he walks. A straight 'A' kid with nine 'O' grades, five Highers and an offer from Glasgow University in his pocket. All this and a kiss from Clorinda too. A song pops into his mind ‘I'm doing all right, getting good grades, The future's so bright, I gotta wear shades!’ Of course, Ben reflects, that’s really when it all goes wrong.

Father Degen's Advice

Terri Eynon

'What if I'd got here earlier, Doc? Just an hour mebbe? Could we have saved her?'

It was a familiar question, but Jack Adcock's honest face was strangely pale. A routine post-hoc discussion, Dr Terence thought to himself, just the wrong setting.

'Who knows, Jack. But what I want to know is this. Why were you up here at all?'

'A nice little earner it was meant to be, Doc. I've been taking one of the toffs around the pit. He wanted to go back to see the overground. Now while it's a bit quiet.'

'You mind your language, young Jack,' admonished Dr Terence, but he knew Adcock's position only too well. Pit deputy, responsible for health and safety in the mine. Trusted by both management and workers, usually. And maybe, this being New Year's Day, we'd see that again. But last summer's General Strike had left a bitter taste.

'Young Mr Richard Dupret, you know, the Director's son. I took him round last week, between Christmas and New Year. Showed him all about mining safety, how we deal with accidents and all. Nice enough, for a toff,' he grinned momentarily, before continuing his story in a more suitable tone. 'Me and Len, you know, my new pit-boy, the manager asked us to take Mr Dupret a tour round some of the surface gear. He's already been round

New Lount. Now he's wanting to see the Stephenson shaft and all what we built for the War effort. We was on our way up to the Grange to meet him. A bit of extra cash for us and a day out in the fresh air.'

Fresh air. That's a thought. Today was a bit better than usual, though. The two men stood on the edge of the black pit bank looking out over the Snibston headstocks and the growing town of Coalville where each terraced house coughed its own cloud of smoke into the low winter clouds already drizzling over Bardon Hill.

The manager's house had no view of the pit, being tucked away in a leafy arboretum of its own. And through the trees was a fishing pond. Which was where Jack and Len had found the girl. A woman really. Half in and half out of the water. You couldn't be sure if she'd been falling in or climbing out. Close to death anyway. The Colliery Ambulance team had done their job, got the girl to the house, wrapped her up. By the time Dr Terence had arrived Maggie, the housekeeper, had brought hot water bottles and blankets. Someone had tried giving her brandy. Young Richard, probably. They'd done their best, all of them.

Wrong setting and wrong gender, for Jack at least. They'd both been there enough times, here and in France. A colleague, a friend, a mate, one minute you're laying a fuse, checking a pit-prop, working a seam, or in his own case, strapping a leg, supervising a stretcher. The next you're up to your knees in a funk-hole, digging for dear life. Sometimes you'd win, sometimes you'd lose. But losing a woman. That was different, for Jack anyway. Watching a woman's life-blood seep away, along with her unborn child, you never forgot that. Jack had been at the front, with one of the tunnelling companies, burrowing under No-man's Land, when Annie lost her baby and her life. Another poor sap might have blown himself up after news like that. The Engineers took him off the front and sent him home. Made the excuse, so it was said, that miners were needed back here. But he'd not been the same since. Handsome, if a bit on the short side, he'd have made some girl a good catch, if only he could settle to one.

'Is it the cold makes their eyes go like that?' Adcock asked.

'Like what?'

'All tiny pupils. I'd not seen that. Except down the pit sometimes.'

'I couldn't say,' Dr Terence hedged. He'd not been at a drowning before. Hypothermia wasn't really his area of expertise. Anyway, the coroner would have her soon. He'd decide on the cause of death. It would all come out in the wash.

It was almost a week before the coroner rang. Yes, he had known she was pregnant. Yes, she had asked him if he would help her and of course he'd said no. What kind of doctor did the coroner think he was speaking to? And no, he didn't think she was that desperate. All fairly standard questions and then one he wasn't expecting. Had he kept full notes of the resuscitation? Of course he had. Had he noticed her pupils? Fixed and dilated of course. She was moribund by the time he arrived on the scene. And what about the bruise? What bruise? He hadn't noticed a bruise.

Dr Terence did his Friday morning visits on autopilot, half his mind going over and over that strange conversation. When he got back for lunch, the fresh smell of the egg and cress sandwiches his wife had left on his desk, wrapped in greaseproof paper, were too much to bear. He stuffed them into his coat pocket and walked out of the surgery and into the square. The new Memorial clock now dominated the town, marking the names of the dead. He let his gaze fall, past the old row of miner's cottages, where Fenella had lived with her mother, and on down the Ashby road to where the headstocks, Smokey and Rider, brood over the pit like a pair of mother hens. Should he go there and see for himself? Or was he too late for that as well? On impulse he turned left and strode up the High Street, away from the pit.

It was peaceful in Coalville Park, the obelisk glinting in the winter sunlight. Erected in 1912, the lettering said. The whole park and recreation ground handed over to the Coalville Urban Council by the athletic club in 1899. He'd have been a baby himself then. Kinder times than these.

'A penny for them.'

'Oh, it's you, Father Degen. I wasn't expecting—'

'None of us were,' Fr Degen replied. They both stood for a minute, pretending to read the inscription, each waiting for the other to speak. Dr Terence was the first to break the silence.

'She was one of yours as well then?'

'Her and her mother. It's been hard on her, you know. Fenella was an only child and the mother a widow. Took in boarders, as so many do.'

'Was one of them the father?'

'Her mother doubts it. Says her daughter had standards.'

'Who else then?'

‘She’d been seeing a lot of Harry Weston, you know, the young gardener at Snibston Grange. He took her to the miner’s gala last September by all accounts.’

‘That would fit with the dates,’ Dr Terence replied, before checking himself. Was it still confidential, now she was dead, he wondered. The miner’s gala, hardly a den of iniquity. He’d been there himself, come to think of it. Had he seen Fenella there? Harry Weston had been in his element of course, judging the vegetable show, marking up the flowers. Coleorton Hall was the perfect venue, what with Wordsworth’s Winter Garden and all. It was kind of Sir George Beaumont to allow them. Miners and their families came from all the pits around, wearing their best finery, to listen to the colliery bands and lark about on the lawns.

‘But how would Harry have got hold of the stuff?’ he murmured to himself.

‘What stuff?’ asked Fr Degen.

‘Oh, I was just working things out in my head.’

‘I can keep confidences too,’ said the priest, kindly. So, there, by the obelisk, Dr Terence told him about the coroner’s call. How angry he’d felt. As if he’d have injected a girl and not written it up in his notes. How the Colliery Ambulance team had told the coroner about her pin-point pupils and the coroner had spotted the small haematoma (a bruise, he explained to the priest) and needle mark in her left antecubital fossa (the inside of the elbow, you know, where you can find a vein).

‘I see,’ said Fr Degen. ‘I agree it is strange. But it sounds as if someone meant her to die.’

‘And the Police Inspector, whatever his name is, has already been to the medical room at the mine. There’s a vial of morphine missing and no record as to where it was used.’

‘But how would young Harry have got hold of it?’

‘I really have no idea.’

Dr Terence was glad when Saturday morning surgery was over. If it stayed fine, he could get out in the garden and finish marking out his seedbeds. If he was quick, he’d just have time to pick up some string and pegs in Leonard Coleman’s shop before it shut for lunch.

‘It’s a rum do, Doc,’ said Leonard. ‘I suppose you’ve heard? They’ve arrested Jack Adcock.’

‘I did hear it, Leonard. The Inspector came and told me. Adcock’s the only one, being a pit deputy, who’d be able to get his hands on a vial of morphine.’

‘They reckon he must have fathered the child as well,’ Leonard added before Rosie butted in.

Rosie by nature as well as by name, she was never the type to interrupt her elders and betters. Which may be why her employer hadn’t sent her to the back of the shop earlier, to stop her earwigging on a private conversation.

‘Please Dr Terence. You’ve got to tell the truth!’

‘What truth?’ Dr Terence managed to ask, pegs and string in one hand, the other holding on to the counter as Mr Coleman bustled out from behind the till and, a few minutes early, closed up the shop.

So that was where Dr Terence heard the rest of the story. Yes, Harry Weston did take Fenella Smith to the Miners' Gala. But he didn't fancy her.

'She's not exactly his type,' Rosie said, before Leonard gave her a hard stare that made her blush. 'All he cares for is flowers.'

As Rosie explained it, Harry had took Fenella to the gala last year 'cause she was smitten with Master Dupret, the young gentleman who'd been at the Beaumont's last summer. He'd gone back to Oxford for Michaelmas but Rosie'd known, afore Christmas, Fenella had caught. She'd told Fenella to see the young Master and ask him to do something. It was Harry Weston had taken her billy-do's up the Hall and met with Dupret. Said he needed to look over the Winter Garden or summat. He'd brought a note back. Dupret said he'd bring an injection, a new thing from London, to get rid of the baby. Fenella had gone up Snibston Grange. To meet him there, early, on New Year's Day.

'Please Dr Terence. No-one will listen to the likes of me. You've got to tell Inspector Lee. If you don't then Jack Adcock will hang, sure as eggs is eggs.

***

'They passed it, you know.'

'Passed what?' Dr Terence looked up from his pile of prescriptions, pen poised expectantly over the pad.

'The Abortion Act. Last night,' replied Dr Sheila Lee.

‘Well, well!’ And, looking into her flushed face, it all came back in a rush. ‘What if,’ he murmured half to himself, ‘what if they’d passed it earlier? Could we have saved her?’

‘Saved who?’

‘Fenella. A case. Oh, it was a long time ago. Way before your time. I was the young enthusiastic doctor then. Gosh, it must be forty years ago now.’ And there was something about the way she looked at him, the way some lady doctors have, that made him tell, in a way he never had before and never would again, the whole sorry tale from beginning to end.

‘So, what happened to them all?’

‘Jack Adcock lost his job as pit deputy. Gross negligence they said. Allowing a controlled drug off the premises without keeping proper records. But they couldn’t prove murder, according to the Inspector, so the prosecutor dropped the case. The last I heard, an anonymous donor paid his passage to Australia and found him a job in a mine, or so they said. Rosie followed him a year or so after.’

‘What about Harry, the gardener? It wasn’t his child then?’

‘Oh, he never married. He’s what you’d call—’

‘Homosexual?’

‘A confirmed bachelor is what we used to call them.’

‘And Richard Dupret?’

‘Oh, he did alright. Followed his father into business. An iron foundry in Bridesley, Birmingham. But if you think about it, after nearly getting Jack Adcock hanged, he probably did that lad a favour. Free passage to Australia and a better life than most. Fr Degen was very upset by it all, of course. I always thought that must be why he wrote this.' Reaching into his desk he pulled out a yellowing poster. 'You know, I've kept it in this drawer here for nigh on forty years.'

Dr Lee read the title out loud, *Advice for Miss 1927 by Father Joseph Degen, St Saviour's, Coalville Leicester,* then scanned through the rest in silence, biting the inside of her lip, before bursting out,

'Is this real? I mean, honestly?'

'Oh, it's real alright. I just love the bit where he advises young women to *Avoid demoralising dances*, don't you?'

'And what would you want Miss 1927 to keep in her handbag for reference, Dr Terence?' she asked with an impish grin.

'Fr Degen makes a good point when he warns young women not to make themselves cheap *even to a duke's son* though I think I'd have put it more boldly. It's not just aristocrats who have rich and powerful friends.'

Dr Terence watched as Dr Lee got herself ready for a busy round of home visits, ironing the of consultant letters with the heel of her hand before carefully folding and refolding the crumpled sheets and sliding them back into Lloyd George pockets.

'And I'd amend Fr Degen's fashion tips on silk and chiffon,' he added. 'To something a lady doctor would likely approve of: *If you must stay out late of an evening, make sure you're wearing a Dutch cap,* perhaps?'

Disclaimer and Acknowledgements

This story is a work of historically informed fiction. Whilst all the places and some of the people are, or were, real, the events and conversations are figments of the author's imagination.

The manager's house at Snibston Grange no longer stands, though the headstocks 'Smokey' and 'Rider' do. The mine is now a scheduled ancient monument, and you can visit the arboretum in the colliery park in Coalville, at the heart of the National Forest. A young woman did drown in the fishpond on the far side of the manager's house a few years earlier than the date of this fictional story. The fishpond no longer exists and should not be confused with the settling ponds established in the 1950s.

Sir George Beaumont did live at Coleorton Hall and a Miners' Gala did take place once a year. The Hall was later taken over by the National Coal Board. I am not sure if there was a Miners' Gala in the summer of 1926. It is notable that the Durham Miners' Gala was cancelled that year due to the General Strike. After the NCB moved out the Hall was refurbished and is now a gated community of luxury flats.

Leonard Coleman did have an ironmonger's shop on Belvoir Road. Father Degen was a well-loved local priest and really did write a leaflet entitled 'Advice for Miss 1927' which he issued to local young women. Dr Sheila Lee was a GP who began practising in Coalville after WWII and who did much to improve healthcare for women in the area. I hope she will forgive me borrowing her name.

The character Richard Dupret was borrowed from Henry Green's modernist novel, 'Living', first published in 1929 and based on his own experiences as the scion of wealthy industrialists in the 1920s.

Dr Terence is an entirely fictional character not to be confused with the real Drs Andrew and Lorna Torrance who practised in the village of Hugglescote in the mid-twentieth century.

Background information was drawn from the work of Jeanne Carswell and Tracey Roberts, *Getting the Coal: impressions of a twentieth century mining community*, published by the Mantle Oral History Project 1992. Any similarity to the actual activities of people kind enough to allow their stories to be recorded is both unintentional and unlikely.

Thanks are due to Stuart Warburton of Coalville Heritage Society for his comments on the historical elements. Any errors that remain are the author's alone.

From ***Christmaston***

Dumitru Langham

We all love Christmas! I mean it's a time where even the grown-ups can act like big…well like big kids. A time for forgiving and for forgetting.

It is a time when you can believe in magic. It's a time where magical memories are created from when you share your first Christmas with your family to the moment you open your long-awaited presents. More importantly it's time to catch up with those you hardly meet and share moments as a family, as well as sitting for hours looking at grandad and grandma's two million photos of grandad in his Speedos. It's time when you can think stuffing to the diet and be merry.

Yet there is something you might wonder or have stopped to wonder; how do your Christmas presents get there in the first place? … well, I am sure you're reading this and thinking why would I think about it at all? It's Christmas time and I am more interested in present opening than thinking about where they came from. Well, you're quite right so let this author do the thinking for you!

So, we've all heard of Santa Claus and his nine magical reindeer, delivering your Christmas presents in one night! But Santa is only one part of this massive snowball of a military operation. There are others involved too and I am not just talking about his army of elves. But seriously have you ever actually stopped to consider how does he do it; ha, ha, well, Santa's lips are certainly tightly sealed, and he is not going to give way his secrets that easily. I mean, that is just being plain rude, just as rude as asking for brussel sprouts! So, let's start from the very beginning.

The tale I am going tell you, is as equally fantastical and even more mystical than stories of the great man himself but we are not going to leave the big guy in the cold snow just yet.

I suppose our story starts like any other Christmas story you might have heard of. It starts with a child…a child writing out a Christmas list for Santa Claus. A child sitting in a chair in their room trying to rack their tiny brains for what they wanted. So many amazing toys they have seen throughout the year... oh, decisions, decisions, decisions. It could be that amazing robot dog they saw while on a summer holiday in Devon; oh, wait that's so last century, or maybe it could be that toy or even that Apple iPhone they wanted while in the Apple store, the thing they wanted so much that they begged their poor parents for it. So many toys to pick, so many to choose from. You couldn't fit them all on one list.

Okay, so…once you've completed your list, it's time for you to go downstairs to show your parents; this is the part, where you will possibly see their faces of either joy or fear when they see what you've written on your wish list for Santa. You could see their brains working like cogs in a clock, trying to work how they are going to complete their task and in secret.

Okay, it's time to send him that Christmas list. That's right kids! It's time to send the letter to Santa! You're probably reading this right now and thinking, Really? Letters? I mean who on earth sends letters in this day and age? Okay, let me rephrase that- I mean some of you might want to send your letters to Santa just to keep tradition going. But nowadays, you kids are more up to date with newer methods of sending Santa's Christmas letter; whether it's via an email, a Facebook message, a tweet, a WhatsApp message or an Instagram post there is more than one way to get your message to the big guy.

It's more likely that for a lot of you especially for you, young ones that your parents will be the ones who actually do the sending. The fact is; it's got to get there, somehow; so, whether it's you or your parents that send the list via social media or traditional mail. It will get there.

Then, I am sure you kids know what's coming next... yes.... the long...lonnggg...wwwwait. It's like a song that you can't get out of your head. You can't sleep; you are always checking your phone or calendar; you are checking it twice. Thinking why, why is it taking so long for Santa to answer my email or letter? You might be wondering what is actually happening behind the scenes? Well let's add a bit of Christmas magic to this story.

So, we've all heard of Santa's amazing workshops in the North Pole. This is the place where he actually makes the toys to send to some of the magical factories in the world, home of some the most delicious sweats; candy and chocolates you would ever taste! Some of these factories could certainly give Willy Wonka a run for his golden ticket. Yet they are the tales of traditional stories you might read in other books or you've seen on a Christmas post card, a film or even a TV show. As this writer hinted, Santa has a mega-operation to complete with a dash of glitter...oh.. this writer has forgotten to tell you that Santa has wizardry-like powers which is true, but he does it in such a subdued way you wouldn't even know it was magic! Even if it flashed right in front of your eyes.

Now this is the part where I can start to reveal some of the true secrets of how the big guy himself achieves this operation....

So, the presents that you have wanted all year are hopefully on their way but you might want to know who else is helping Santa? I mean come on this guy and his army of elves can't do it all by themselves? Even Santa would need help. But you might be thinking…. err…doesn't Santa have magical powers? He could do things that no normal person, could ever dream of; Well magic doesn't solve everything you know! I can exclusively reveal that your parents are involved with Santa! Dum, dum, daaaa! That's right! Kids, your parents! Their secret is out at last! They are involved with helping Santa to get ready for the big night! Yes, they are one part of the secret mission of Christmas.

Have you ever accidentally wandered into your living room and seen your parents acting shiftily; talking quietly, not making eye contact and stopping instantly as you entered a room as though someone had switched off their voice box like turning off Christmas fairy lights; how all of sudden they would avoid awkward questions that you would throw at them like,

"Oh, we were… we were just arranging a few items for the Christmas tree which we're going to pick up next week." But you are not fooled because the Christmas trees is already up. So, they'll try with something else, like;

"Dang, we only just remembered granddad's present so If you could be kind enough to leave the room as you might accidently tell granddad." In which case you would probably see your mum elbowing your dad to shut him up for fear that he might give the game away. Then your dad would hastily change it to grandma saying;

"Oh no it's not granddad's present it's grandmas present, we were meaning to order her a new pair of glasses and a hearing aid. She's forever losing her glasses and hearing aids…oh I think she lost her twentieth set of hearing aids…err, again so we're going to get her a pair which she can't lose so easily." Okay… okay... I think you are getting the idea. I think it's time to see how your parents really help out Santa in getting your toys to the North Pole before Christmas eve.

Just how much truth is there in the existence of Santa? This is probably the part where you are yelling at the book, of course he's real, he's Santa Claus; just as real as I am, your imaginary narrator who will help you while you read this enthralling tale, that you or your parents have kindly bought off Amazon or from your local bookstore; which keeps this writers bills paid. But enough of that, it's time to sit back, relax and enjoy this tale of a mysterious man who is as stealthy as a ninja from your Lego set and has the ability to deliver your Christmas presents with the help of magical reindeers all in one night. So, you might ask why this writer is questioning the existence of Santa Claus, I mean that just as rude as offering you fruit salad instead of a nice chocolate bar! Yet, why hasn't anyone seen Santa or reported anything? If Santa is as real as they make him out to be then how come no one has been able to find him?

Well, you might be shocked to know that Santa gets about quite a bit. If you've heard ever the lyrics, *"he sees when you are sleeping, he knows when you've been bad or good so be good for goodness sake."* In other words, he really knows what you are doing even if you don’t. I mean how does he know what you want for Christmas when he’s never even seen your list or you?

Well unfortunately there is a term I like to say which is a magician never reveals his tricks and it’s the same with the big man himself. Let’s see if we can unwrap how Santa knows what you want for Christmas; how many old guys you see with beards like Santa; old men that make you do double take! I suppose you could say these old bearded Santa Claus look like spies for Santa and are somehow relaying information to the big man himself. okay So, let start from the beginning; allllll…tttthee wwway back!

Chapter 17- About Us

About Fliss Middleton

Fliss Middleton lives in Leicestershire, England where she writes at her neighbours dining table. She is the proud grandmother of fifteen grandchildren and great grandchildren. At other times, she sells cards, plays scrabble and walks her large rescue dog. Her writing is a quaint mishmash of children's stories, poetry, short fiction and memoirs.

About Peter Huckerby

Peter is a founder member of the Coalville Writers Group and has lived in North West Leicestershire since 1999. His career has centred around high street retail visual merchandising both here in the U.K. and internationally. His book *Easy Visual Merchandising* is available on Amazon Kindle. Peter is a keen photographic artist and has work displayed in Saatchi Art. He dedicates much of his spare time to imaginative pursuits in conceptual art and creative writing. His inspiration emanates from everyday life…yet slightly out of kilter.

About D J Gilmour

Douglas Gilmour grew up in Balloch, Helensburgh and the Isle of Lewis before a stint at Glasgow University. He then went south to seek fame and fortune. After various adventures in the

Berkshire Badlands he settled in Leicestershire where people still have the time to talk to strangers. He is lucky enough to be married with two sons but sadly his dog can no longer walk him back from the pub.

He has two books available on Amazon:

Remnant Kings is a Vampire novel set in Scotland in 1625. https://www.amazon.co.uk/dp/1502301385/

Rocket Surgery is an entirely made-up story about a lad who grows up in the West of Scotland and runs off to join the electronics industry. https://www.amazon.co.uk/dp/1542995388/

Hooded Crow, his third book should be out before the end of 2022 and has been described as 'superb' by one of the beta readers so might just be worth the wait.

About Cerys Linton

After losing the capacity to read, Cerys felt it would be reasonable to start to write. She feels that, for her, writing is a helpful way to process life experiences, by pouring them in to a mental magimix, or squeezing them into a fun-factory of the mind, from whence strange shapes are extruded that bear little or no relationship to the original experiences. But still, she finds it helpful. People write for many different reasons, which can also change, but a good reason to start is that it can be fun.

About Rosemary Blake

Rosemary has lived in Leicestershire for over 30 years. She trained in Adult Education and Mental Health and worked in the charity sector. She and her partner have 3 sons and 6 grandchildren.

Rosemary often made-up bedtime stories for her grandchildren, but she hadn't considered writing until she was off work with an injured shoulder. This meant sitting upright day and night until it set. She was inspired by an Open University writing course.

She says, 'I write to play, creating a world that I have ordered to suit my whim. A friendly world where people sort out their problems and learn from them. Writing feels equally like using modelling clay and like chewing over a word game.'

Her first novels were set in the early 1970s as a way of highlighting changes in society. Writing allows her to draw on memories of Nottinghamshire and of places that she's visited. She explores a wide range of issues: discrimination, group dynamics, feminism, the history of gay rights, prostitution and people trafficking.

This all sounds very heavy, but she wraps it in the fancy trappings of women's fiction/chicklit. You can find out more about her five novels on www.rosemaryblake.co.uk

Feeling isolated during the pandemic, Rosemary went online to the Leakey Pens writing group, Birmingham LGBT+ writers, and of course, Coalville Writers Group. She also signed up to writing classes with the Workers Education Association where she learned to pare away unnecessary words. The tutor there encouraged the class to enter flash fiction writing competitions.

Her latest novel *Rosy's Recycling Tea Shop* is of the chick lit genre and is set in modern day Somerset. Rosemary is not the Rosy of the title, although she does have experience of working in a recycling project.

In the future she will concentrate on writing more short stories, although she is interested in the Anglo Saxons and this may develop into a future novel. Anglo-Saxon chick lit anyone?

About Terri Eynon

A founder member of the Coalville Writers Group, Terri moved to Coalville temporarily in 1994. She occasionally published poems in small magazines whilst earning herself an NHS pension. Terri took time to study a Masters in Literary Linguistics at Nottingham University and returned to the Writers Group early 2022. She now works for The Reader to share stories and poems in criminal justice settings. She is the Chair of Snibston Heritage Trust and a volunteer proofreader for community organisations.

The name is Dumitru Langham,

aspiring writer. Urban contemporary fantasy is my speciality. If you haven't got elves, dwarves, or dragons then I am not writing about it. I do sometimes dive into the realm of science fiction, but fantasy is my main area.

My current job is an assistant estate man at SMB group and previously I was a media technician.

But let's go back to 1989, the end of the era of 80s electric music and the birth of cheesy party music with the rise of boy bands and girl band power; also known for the Berlin wall and the fall of communism in Europe. Romania emerged from behind the iron curtain of communism after killing Nicolae Ceausescu the Voldemort, the Darth Sidious, of dictatorship. Romania is known as the home of the vampire Count Dracula, but the thing that many people don't know about is the orphanages of Romania. That's where I and my unknown brother were sent.

Like Oliver Twist our outlook was black and very hopeless. It was especially bleak for me as I was diagnosed with HIV/AIDS due to an infected blood transfusion. Okay, so that's the sad part over, now let's shift up a gear and meet what I like to call our guardian angel or hero, mum Ruth Langham. She came to Romania and found me, which was lucky because I only had 3 months to live because everyone was so terrified of being turned into a mutant zombie if they touched me. But thank to mum's amazing strong spirit she found me and with the help of her and the generous people of Coalville, £8,000 was raised for me to have surgery. Then not long after my surgery we found my brother who had had life a bit rougher and longer in the Ceausescu's hotel aka the orphanage. He joined the Langham clan, and we were adopted, and the rest is history. Our mum very sadly died before her time of cancer. So that's the history lesson done!

Ever since I was small and could talk, I used to tell stories, usually about my favourite Saturday morning cartoon, 'Scooby Doo', normally to my nana Joy, a published writer who wrote a book about me and my brother's story. Apart from my amazing family, my mentors and amazing teachers, Jon Holmes, and James West, bless them, put up with me pitching all my fantastical ideas for possible film or tv productions. Jon, James, and a few others thought that my ideas for scripts would make amazing children's books. So that's how I decided to aim more towards novel writing rather than the silver screen.

Macy Milldale

has being working as a mental health nurse for over 30 years. When becoming a part time empty nester, she joined the writing group. Initially considering writing a self-help book for building self-esteem, she then incorporated self-help material into a chick-lit. She hopes to publish *New Year Newish Me* in 2023. When not writing she enjoys dog walking with her husband, reading and her favourite thing is long conversations with friends in coffee shops.

K H Parks

Writer K H Parks speaks 3 languages and has taught English in France and Spain. Her travels have also taken in Quebec and Ontario in Canada and New England in the USA where she served on a children's holiday camp. She has worked in export sales, accounts, administration and more recently as a course trainer and private tutor. She lives in Leicestershire with her family. Her hobbies, besides creative writing and proofreading, include English literature, theatre, cinema and walking and cycling in the countryside.

Kelly O'Shea

I am an aspiring writer. I am a fan of horror, crime and mystery. I have an open mind on all things in life and a more unusual take on death, having spent the last 10 years of my life working as a paranormal investigator. Yes, it's a real job and yes I got paid! Mostly because I was self-employed so naturally, I paid myself! I like to use some of the experiences from my past to create horror stories that make you feel, laugh and enter a strange new world.

I am working on a series of short stories and a novel. All due to come out in 2023, all being well and confidence not failing me.

I am a mom of two amazing children. I unfortunately had to close my business as Covid continued and decided to head to university as a mature student, fulfilling a lifelong ambition. I am studying zoology, but my interest lies in medicinal and poisonous plants and fungi.

Printed in Great Britain
by Amazon

11781951R00082